Bridget [Blankley] ... Nigeria. She worked as an ... full-time carer before coming late to writing; her first piece of fiction was published in her early 50s. Her fiction, however, has since gone on to win several prizes including 2013 Winchester Writing Can be Murder and Commonword Children's Writing Competition 2016. I[n the] same year, she was runner up for the Thomas [Gr]ay Anniversary Poetry Competition as well as runner [up for] the 2017 Alpine Fellowship Writing Prize.

[Bridge]t has an autism spectrum disorder (ASD) and is [delig]hted to support the work of The National Autistic [Societ]y with the publication of *The Ghosts & Jamal*. [Bridge]t lives in Southampton. @BridgetBlankley [bridge]tblankley.com

The Ghosts & Jamal

Bridget Blankley

HopeRoad Publishing
PO Box 55544
Exhibition Road
London SW7 2DB

First published in Great Britain by HopeRoad 2018
Copyright © 2018 Bridget Blankley

A CIP catalogue record for this book is available from the British Library.

Supported using public funding by
**ARTS COUNCIL
ENGLAND**

ISBN 978-1-908446-63-3
eISBN 978-1-908446-56-5

Printed and bound by TJ International Ltd, Padstow, Cornwall, UK
www.hoperoadpublishing.com

Dedicated to the memory of Gertrude Soemers,
a devoted nurse and wonderful person who helped
me with many of the details connected with Jamal's
illness, and who was always there for me.

Ghosts

It was light when Jamal woke, but no one was up and about. Morning should have been the noisiest, the busiest time of day, but nothing was moving. He sat trying to decide if he was really awake, looking at the walls of the hut, checking that everything was where it ought to be, straining to hear the sounds of the camp. Straining to hear, what? There was nothing to hear. Last night's attack was definitely over and the hut seemed OK, and – even better – Jamal was still alive, so that was all good, but the silence was definitely not good.

If it was light he should hear children squabbling, uncles finishing their prayers and aunties starting breakfast and hushing their babies, but there was nothing. He couldn't even hear the ear-buzzing hum that usually followed the bombs. Everywhere was totally, utterly silent.

Jamal realised just how frightened he was; frightened, but not stupid, so he didn't call out. Instead he sat perfectly still, holding his breath. He didn't know who was outside and he didn't know the reason for the silence, but Jamal was pretty sure that someone out there had caused it. He also knew that he didn't want to meet them. He had no idea what to do next. But he did know that being alone was a bad idea, that calling out was a worse idea and that waiting to be found was the worst idea yet. So he sat very still, trying not to make a noise, trying to disappear into the shadows and trying to be certain of the right direction to take. He was thirteen, almost a man – not that anyone thought so, he was still treated like a baby – but he knew he was a man. A man who could work out what to do.

As he sat there, hardly breathing, the early morning smoke made him sneeze. Jamal froze; had he given himself away? Slowly, he uncrossed his legs, easing the pins-and-needles from his ankles. If anyone was watching they'd know where he was now. He waited, expecting them to come into his hut.

Nothing happened.

He decided to go outside. His hut had been built on an outcrop of rock where the soil was too thin to grow crops. If he went outside he would be able to look down into the family compound and see what was wrong. Jamal pulled a blanket round him – right over his head so his face was hidden. It was an unimportant act – a habit – but that day it would save his life ...

There was too much smoke. It didn't tickle his nose any more, it was grabbing at his throat, squeezing the air into his stomach in wrenching coughs. He was choking, gasping acid breaths till suddenly his ears were bursting with noise. He fell to the ground, his blanket slipping across his twitching body, hiding his face under the heavy cloth. That was when the pick-up drove past.

'This one's gone, boys, or nearly gone. Don't waste the grenades, we're not finished yet.'

The truck accelerated up the hill taking its masked passengers away from Jamal and on to another target.

Jamal's hut was outside the compound. Not far outside – he could still hear the talking, see the children playing and even smell the bread baking on the stones – but it was not part of the village. He was close, but not too close. Jamal was unlucky, marked by spirits, so he wasn't allowed to enter the compound.

He hadn't been abandoned and chased away from the village like his mother. The Imam had seen to that. He told Jamal's family that Jamal was ill and they had a duty to care for him. But his family didn't want Jamal close and as soon as the Imam left they built a hut as far away as they dared and Jamal had lived there ever since. Food was sent out with small children who scampered up the slope to Jamal's hut, skirting in circles to make sure that no shadow from Jamal, or his hut, fell on them. Water was fetched from the well and delivered in much the same way. Overall, although he was excluded from their society, Jamal's family had ensured that he would at least survive.

Now, as Jamal struggled to stand, he looked towards the compound and realised that his family would no longer be able to help him. The thorn hedge that surrounded the compound was intact. The animals were in the corral and his family were scattered about the compound, just where they ought to be. His aunties near the fires, their children clustered by the huts and his uncles in the centre of the compound, gathered around a bright red canister. As far as Jamal could tell, only two things were wrong: a dirty yellow vapour was streaming from the canister and everyone in the compound was dead.

The smoke that made Jamal cough and choke in his hut was partly from the contents of the canister and partly from Auntie Sheema, who had fallen onto the cooking fire. Jamal hesitated; leaving Auntie to burn seemed wrong, but she would not want Jamal to touch her, even to save her from the fire. He wasn't sure what to do. Jamal's life had been simple: to eat what he was given, keep himself clean, sweep his hut and bury his waste. He had a role in the family: he had to draw bad spirits away from the compound and let them feed on him. Thus he would twitch and shake when the spirits came, rolling in dirt or knocking into the walls, while his aunties and uncles and cousins stayed safe. Jamal hated being visited by spirits, but he accepted his lot. The spirits came to him, punished him and made him ill, but they left his family alone.

Today that hadn't happened. Jamal had slept soundly when the spirits came. Ghosts were escaping from the canister and they had killed his family. He stumbled, his eyes burning, smoke and tears stealing his sight. He called out to the ghosts, begging them to leave the compound and to come to him; but the ghosts didn't listen, they just hovered in the hollows, snaking through the huts, hungrily searching for souls. Jamal knew he couldn't help. Soul-seekers had no use for Jamal, he had no soul. His grandfather had told him that, on the day they buried his mother.

He turned away, picked up the can that held his water and shuffled east following the churned tracks that the spirits had left. The yellow smoke from the canister was drifting in that direction. The ghosts must have had their fill. There was no need for them to stay in the compound. Jamal decided to follow them, find out where they were going, or maybe where they lived. That sounded like a good scheme. There was nothing he could do here; maybe he could find the home of the ghosts. But what then? Would they listen to him? And if they did, could he save his family, or had the ghosts already taken their souls?

He had no plan. For as long as he could remember he hadn't needed to plan. His family had cared for him and he had protected his family. Now he had nothing, so he walked. His red blanket and a copy of the Qur'an, which he couldn't read, were the only familiar things in this unfamiliar world. He needed the blanket to hide from the ghosts. He wasn't quite sure why he needed the Qur'an, but the Imam had told him to keep it by his side, and the Imam was a nice man. He would come to the hut and talk to Jamal, and sometimes he would shave the hair from his head so it didn't itch. *Yes,* Jamal thought, *the Imam is a good man, so I shall take the book with me, to please him.*

A Walk Across the Sand

Jamal was hungry. His family had died before breakfast so nothing had been brought up to his hut. He knew that the aunties picked plants to put in the stews, but they had never taken Jamal with them. He didn't know which plants he should eat so he didn't eat any, just in case they made him sick. But he was so hungry that when he passed a bush covered in red berries he thought that being sick might be better than being hungry. He was about to pick the fruit when he saw that there were dead birds in the bush, six of them. It was strange because there were no flies round the birds and no ants on their bodies. But Jamal didn't think about the flies, not till much later. He just decided to leave the berries, even though they looked sweet. The birds might have been attacked by the ghosts or the berries might have been poisonous –

Jamal didn't know. But he didn't want to risk the fruit killing him as well. He kept walking.

Maybe he could find another family. A family who were plagued by spirits and who would look after him if he kept the ghosts away. Jamal thought that would be his best plan. He would have to go a long way from home though, because if they heard that his family had died they wouldn't allow him to stay. That was too much bad luck for a boy to bring with him. He kept walking, following the tracks in the dust until the sun was high. He had never been this way before, not on his own. He wondered if he should have stayed at home and forgotten about finding the ghosts' home.

He could see a compound about an hour's walk away. There were no signs of people – no smoke, no goats, nothing. It looked abandoned, or worse, but Jamal needed help, so he pushed through the scrub towards the huts. The spirit tracks were less clear, but they were still there. Wherever the red dust broke through the rocks Jamal could see the tracks. He shivered a little and the air seemed to stick in his chest, whistling and wheezing to escape as he forced each breath. He felt as if one of the spirits had its hand on his shoulder, pushing him to the ground. So he pulled his blanket across his face, breathing the familiar smells of wool and smoke, keeping the ghosts away from his mouth. He wanted to reach the compound – there would be water there – but between him and the compound were more ghosts. They were snaking up the hill towards him and Jamal knew he needed to leave before the ghosts smothered him like they'd smothered everyone else. He struggled, trying to stand, taking one step then another, trying to escape into the fresh air while all the time the ghosts were grabbing at him, pulling him back to where everything had died. The comforting taste of his mother's blanket between his teeth seemed to protect him as he forced his legs forward. Step, stagger, stumble, step, fall, stand – slowly escaping back up the hill where the ghosts couldn't reach him. When he couldn't walk any more, he sat, leaning his back against a tree.

What was it doing there, standing on its own with nothing growing around it? Jamal might have spent time trying to work out why the tree hadn't been cut down, but he didn't; he was too tired and too thirsty. He drank the last of his water and closed his eyes. He knew he shouldn't sleep – he was out in the open, away from the fires and the thorn fences that keep the animals away – but he'd been walking for so long and it was so quiet that he just wanted to sleep. He felt warm and comfortable and he wrapped his mother's blanket around him to keep the flies from his face. But there were no flies. Jamal stopped feeling tired. There were always flies: even at night when the brown flies slept, the mosquitos came. Suddenly the tree didn't feel safe any more. He wasn't sure why – it was something to do with the flies, but he couldn't quite work out what. But he knew he had to go and find somewhere safer.

The tree was tall – taller than the trees near home – but it had thick branches, even low down. Jamal thought that he'd be able to see a long way from the top of this tree. He tried to climb, but he needed both hands. He was forced to leave his Qur'an behind. He wondered what the Imam would say; he had told Jamal to keep it with him, to look after it like a new-laid egg, and now he was planning to go without it. Jamal said to himself that it would be OK to leave the book on the ground, as long as he could see where it was. He put the book a little way from the tree and started to climb. It was no use: he still couldn't get further than the first branch. He couldn't climb and keep his blanket wrapped around him. It slipped from his shoulders and twisted itself round his ankles. He nearly fell. So he dropped the blanket. Jamal was wearing blue shorts, the ones his cousin had outgrown. He had never climbed trees, but he knew his cousin could climb – Jamal had watched him from the corner of his hut. *If Ham can climb then I can climb,* thought

Jamal. *After all, I must be as big as he was, if I am wearing his shorts.*

Jamal decided that he would climb every tree he passed from then on – there weren't many on the plain – and stopping at each tree would make the journey seem shorter. He pulled himself through the branches, clinging tightly as his feet slipped, even when the thorns ripped the skin on his hands. It was strange, the higher he climbed the fewer thorns there were. It was like a stockade to keep people away from the sky he thought, as he reached a strong forked branch near the top of the tree. Sitting there he could see everything, the whole world – or at least he imagined it must be the whole world. He could see the plain that he had walked across and he could see that the land began to rise ahead of him. It kept rising to where there were more trees. Beyond the trees there were rocks and beyond the rocks was a mountain. Jamal had never seen mountains before, not close up, only their blue-grey line on the horizon. This mountain was a bit different; it wasn't part of a line of mountains. It stood on its own. It was as if a giant had thrown a calabash when he'd finished drinking and it had stuck, neck down in the green land. Of course, he didn't believe in giants. They were not like witches or the bog trolls that lived by the river and pulled careless children under the water. Giants were just made-up things to make little children behave, but still, this mountain looked odd, a great grey boulder rising out of the plain. Jamal was sure that there was something special about it. There had to be. So special that an important man like his grandfather would choose to live there.

He had heard his uncles talking about a mountain without God. He was not sure what that meant – how could God be kept from a mountain, or anywhere else? The Imam had told him that God was everywhere and knew everything. His Qur'an would have the answers, he was sure of that. The Imam had said that all the answers to the questions of man were there. 'But what is the good of answers that are hidden?' he would ask his grandfather. Surely a man like his grandfather would have learnt to read.

There was something else about the mountain, he was sure there was. Something that he was meant to remember. He would think about that when he was walking to the mountain. Thinking about the mountain would stop him remembering his aunties and their fish soups and groundnut stews – red with chillies and tomatoes. His mouth watered when he thought of fatty palm weevils, crisply fried crickets and – when the rains came – nutty termites with maize pudding. He shook his head, trying to drive thoughts of food away. But he imagined he could smell smoky roast goat. He couldn't, of course. There were no goats – and no one to cook them. But when you're hungry and alone it's easier to imagine your favourite food than to remember that your favourite things have all gone.

'Think about the mountain,' he said aloud. 'Think about climbing that enormous mountain.' His voice sounded too quiet in the empty air and he slid down the tree, grabbing at branches. It was much harder to climb down than it had been to climb up. He was nearly at the bottom. There was one more branch to go when he heard the ghosts hissing in his ears. They must have seen him sitting in the tree and been waiting till he climbed down. He should have kept his blanket so he could have hidden. And he should have kept quiet instead of shouting out loud. Jamal smelt their breath and felt them push his chest and pinch his nose. Then he fell from the tree.

The ghosts must have just wanted to tease him by reminding him that they were there. Because they left him quickly. When he sat up it was still light and still quiet. He felt sick, like he always did, and very thirsty and his belly grumbled with hunger. But there was no water left to drink and no food in his pockets. He would just have to stay thirsty till he reached the mountain and he could find his grandfather. He was very sore. His back ached and he could feel the blood where the branches had scratched at his skin. His wrist was sore too. Very sore. He could hardly move it. He would have to tie his blanket round his neck, and use his good hand to carry the Qur'an. There was even blood on his blue shorts. When he found some water he would wash them, or flies would smell the blood and land on his legs.

He looked up at the tree. It had been good to climb, as good as anything he had ever done. It had not been so good to fall, but he would recover. All in all, he thought, it was worth the fall, just to have climbed the tree.

He turned towards the mountain, away from where he had come, away from home. He had thought about walking to the mountain and now he would do it, although it looked a long way away and the sun would set soon. So he would have to start walking tomorrow. He wished that he had a fire and a bowl of Auntie's stew, and enough thorns to make a fence, but he had nothing. Being next to a tree was better than being alone on the plain so he wrapped himself in his blanket and slept, his head on his book so that he was as close to it as he could be.

In the morning, he was cold and stiff. He could hardly move his left wrist, and soil and twigs had stuck to the cuts on his back. He tried to pick at the scabs to clean them, but he couldn't reach. *I must get to a river and wash,* he thought. But he didn't want to think about the river, because when he did, he remembered that he wanted a drink. He knew he had to get to the mountain. There would be water there. Jamal wasn't certain how he knew but he was quite sure.

As he eased himself up he saw that the leaves were damp. Jamal thought about eating the leaves – there were no dead birds on this tree – but he was scared they might be poisonous. He knew many trees made poison to keep the grubs from eating them. He decided to get as much water as he could from the leaves and drink that. *The water won't be poisoned,* he thought. It wasn't, but there was only half a mouthful, hardly enough to wet his tongue. He felt even more thirsty than he did before.

I have to get to the mountain, Jamal thought, *or I'll die*, and there was no point in leaving home just to die somewhere else.

Jamal started to walk, thinking, *I need to get to Grandfather.* And that was all he thought about as he walked. He stopped thinking about the scratches on his legs or his sore wrist or how hungry he felt. Every step was a step closer to his grandfather and that was the only thing he had to remember. When his grandfather had come to the compound he had told Jamal that he lived two days' walk away, on the Mountain Without God. Was this the right mountain? Jamal knew that he should go to the mountain; he knew he had to find somewhere to live. He just hoped that he'd found the right mountain.

Jamal couldn't actually remember much about his grandfather, or why he had left Jamal with his aunties instead of taking him back to the mountain, but that didn't matter. Jamal had somewhere to go. And there was someone who would look after him and help him to find where the ghosts lived.

Although he had to stop three times to sit down because he was feeling dizzy, he reached the rocks before the sun was overhead. He might have stayed where he was and forgotten about the mountain if it hadn't been for his grandfather. Jamal just knew that his grandfather would be waiting for him somewhere on the mountain.

The rocks were flat and smooth. Jamal hadn't realised this when he saw them from the tree. Also, there were paths between them. Paths worn by hundreds of feet crossing them over hundreds of years. It was cooler here too. There were more trees and more shade, and Jamal could even hear a river, although he couldn't see it. The path twisted and snaked like a liana stretching between the trees. Jamal was in a hurry, but he was too weak to clamber over the rocks. He followed the path. It was the slowest way to climb, only rising one step for every five or six, but it was easy. Old people, sick people, fat mammies and small babies, they all used the steps while the young and the strong clambered over the rocks. He wanted to stay on the path.

The steps seemed welcoming, but they weren't; the ghosts had been here too. They were gone now, those soul-seekers. Right in front of Jamal, before the steps really started, they had left one of their red canisters. But the ghosts had gone – none of the yellow trails or choking odours remained. But they had definitely been here.

Jamal hesitated. He wanted to examine the red canister – to know more about the ghosts and what they were looking for. He also wanted to stay alive. Was there a ghost still in the canister, waiting for the others to return? Maybe waiting for another soul. After all, everyone else who had been here was dead, their souls had already gone. But Jamal didn't have a soul, so he would be safe. He needed to know, but he was afraid to know. He stood rocking backwards and forwards, not sure what to do next.

He sat down, feeling alone, wanting to cry. It was unfair; he wanted to cry but he was too thirsty, his body wouldn't waste water on tears. He decided that he would cry later, and maybe scream and shout and throw rocks at trees. Just so everyone, the old Gods and the spirits and the ghosts and the God in his book would all know that he was being treated unfairly. But before he could do any of these things he would have to find something to drink. And before that, he would look at the red canister. This was where the ghosts lived. If Jamal wanted to stop the ghosts, he would have to find out why they had come. He knew that any ghost left in the canister would kill him, but it was time to be brave, to be a man. If Allah willed it, Jamal would die. If he did not, Jamal would live and maybe stop the ghosts from killing anyone else.

Jamal edged forward, tapping the canister with a stick. It rolled away, reached the edge of the first step then stopped, as if the ghost inside was deciding what to do next. Jamal held his breath and waited. It toppled onto the soil. The sound, bell-like and innocent, echoed across the mountains. The ring reminded Jamal of a single, lonely cicada. One sound when there should have been hundreds.

Secrets and Stories

J amal took a step towards the canister – not too close, but close enough to see inside. As it rolled, smoke slid lazily onto the soil like a small blind snake slipping under a stone. It wasn't ordinary smoke – the colour was wrong. Jamal knew how to change smoke – burning goat skins made it dark and burnt button weeds made it go yellow and smell of ants – but he didn't know how you'd make smoke this colour. It was the colour of an old man's pee. He wondered if this was the colour of dying. The ghosts killed people, and the old men he'd met had all died. Even his mum's eyes, when she died, had been yellow like the smoke. He'd looked at her eyes and he'd wanted to close them, but his uncles wouldn't let him. They had shooed him away, whispering to each other when they thought he wasn't listening.

It was after his mum died and his grandfather left, taking all the palm wine from his uncle's store, that everyone told Jamal that he was unlucky. That was when they built his hut right away from the compound.

His eyes began to prickle, not from the smoke that was sneaking down the hill, slipping through the cracks and into the ground. No, this time his eyes were stinging with tears. He sat on the step, digging little holes in the soil with his stick.

'Stupid ghosts.' His voice sounded like a radio turned up too loud, distorted and crackly. He couldn't even shout. How would anyone know he was here if he could only whisper? Jamal looked around. It didn't matter – there was no one here. Even the ghosts had better places to be.

'No time to feel sorry for yourself, Jamal,' he said. 'That was then, this is now. You are not a boy, crying like a baby.' It worked, he knew what he had to do. He wiped his nose on his arm and went back to where the cylinder had landed.

He bent down, looking at it closely. The first thing he noticed was that it wasn't completely red. It had signs and marks all over it, writing too. But the writing wasn't clear and anyway, Jamal couldn't read. He understood the pictures though. Pictures were there to tell stories, like the pictures on the shops in town – the man having his hair cut at the barber's shop and the steaming cup painted on the wall of the teashop. You didn't need words when there were pictures. There was a fish on the cylinder. A fish with a line through it. Not a very good fish, more like the carvings that children make, or the beads that you sometimes found hidden in the soil. It was definitely meant to be a fish but Jamal was not sure why it was crossed out. Was it bad for fish, or made from fish? Perhaps the cross was meant to be a fishing net.

There were other pictures too: a tree, some bones and another cross. It was an odd mix of images. What was the story? Maybe if you caught fish in a net, then the ancestors who lived in the trees would be angry. Maybe if you didn't catch fish then the ghosts would come and haunt the trees. Or were the ghosts looking for fish, or trees or bones? What good were pictures if they didn't make sense?

Jamal decided that these pictures were meant to confuse. The ghosts had secrets and they wanted only the right people to understand them. Jamal knew that he wasn't one of the right people. He was too unimportant to be the sort of person ghosts would want to share their stories with. Then he remembered his grandfather. It was time to find him.

His aunties had said that Jamal's grandfather was a powerful man. They were all afraid of him. If he was very powerful and if Jamal could find him, maybe he would understand the story on the canister. If he knew what story was being told, maybe he could give the ghosts what they were looking for. Then they might go away.

So, Jamal had two – no, three – problems that he needed to solve before he could even think about finding the ghosts.

First, he needed to find water. He needed to do that before he did anything else. After that, he needed to find something that would hold the red canister. It was too heavy to carry up the mountain in his arms, and he was not as good at balancing things on his head as his aunties were.

Then he had to find Grandfather and that was the hardest thing that he had to do. Because this might not be the right mountain, and even if it were, it looked as though it was covered in caves. And Grandfather could be living in any one of them.

Between Jamal and the top of the mountain were all the people whom the ghosts had killed. He would have to find a way to get around them, or over them. Jamal was pleased that he didn't have to solve that problem quite yet. He would leave the red canister where it was and go hunting for water. There was a stream near the steps that led down to the river, but the fish and the frogs that should have been swimming in it had all died. The birds that had been feeding on the frogs had all died and had fallen into the stream. Jamal wondered if the ghosts were swimming in the river, among the dead things. Even the wriggling mosquito larvae were dead. If the ghosts were so hungry that they had taken the life from mosquitos then they would surely take Jamal's life if he drank from the river. Jamal looked around. There had to be something to drink; there were so many people here, they wouldn't all have been thirsty. There was no market, so the people hadn't come to shop; they'd come to walk up the mountain.

Jamal saw that some people had been selling drinks – Sprite and Fanta in small bottles and juices in packets. He liked Fanta. The Imam would bring bottles of Fanta when he visited, leaving a crate in the compound for his cousins. A whole crate, less one bottle. That bottle he would share with Jamal while Auntie cooked dinner. He licked his lips; they were cracked and sore. The ice had melted but the icebox was full. But Jamal wasn't quite sure what he should do. He needed a drink. He'd finished the water he had brought with him a long time ago, before he had left the spirit tracks. He could fill his bottle from the melted ice, but what if the ghosts had been in the ice? Would the water still be safe to drink?

Jamal wasn't used to being thirsty; there was always water at home – water and *fufu* and stew. He didn't have any money. His uncle had kept everyone's money. He kept it in a tin that he hid under the thorn bushes. Jamal knew where it was, but he hadn't thought to take it, even though Uncle was dead. So Jamal had no money and nothing to sell. He didn't want to take a drink – that would be stealing and he knew that was wrong. But he needed a drink; he needed it very much. He looked at the icebox and the drinks and he looked at the auntie, half fallen from her stool. Now he was worried again. He started rocking, like he did when he needed to think. It was as if he was trying to pull the answers from somewhere deep inside him. But the answers stayed hidden. Jamal wanted someone to tell him what to do. He was unlucky, a spirit boy, not someone who was used to making decisions.

Jamal looked around – the spirits were returning, he was sure of it. He could smell the sweet nutmeg on their breath and hear their voices buzzing in his ears. He leant against a tree trunk, keeping himself hidden, even though he knew the spirits would still find him. He was thinking about the bottles in the icebox when the spirits wound their smoky selves around his eyes and he sank into an uneasy blackness.

The spirits tortured Jamal for most of the day. He woke when the sun had burnt itself out. He woke to something else as well. Flies. There were flies everywhere, filling the air and settling on the bodies. The ghosts must have been satisfied at last. *That's good,* Jamal thought. *I couldn't stop the ghosts from coming but at least I've chased them away. The mountain might come back to life, even if all the people don't.*

Just then Jamal heard swifts chattering at the sudden feast of flies. Other birds would be here soon, and animals too, if they had escaped the ghosts. Jamal had seen the wild dogs fighting over goats and he wanted to be away before they came. He had no time to think, he had to start walking again. He went over to the drink seller. He looked at her. She was covered in flies and their black-tipped eggs. Obviously, she didn't need his money. Even if he caught the ghosts she wouldn't want to be chased back into this body.

He pushed as many drinks as he could into a cloth and tied it, like a lumpy baby, to his back. Then he took one more bottle; it was warm, but he didn't care. He opened the bottle, smiling as the gas escaped, hissing like an angry beetle. Jamal drank the sticky liquid then dropped the bottle and took an extra one to drink on the way. Maybe if another boy came along, he would be able to pick up the bottle and sell it. Maybe that was a way to pay for the drink, leaving the bottle for someone else.

He needed to be able to carry the cylinder so he took a basket from one of the dead aunties, though he had to push her arms to free the bag. He was sure he shouldn't have – he'd been told not to touch other people – but he needed the basket and this auntie wouldn't know that he had pulled at her hands. This was the second time in his life that he had stolen something and it was much easier than the first. When he stole the Fanta he had worried so much that the spirits had heard him and returned. But this time it was easy. He saw the basket in the fat auntie's hand and reasoned that she must have been very wealthy to have grown so fat. Maybe she had several baskets at home and would think it good to give a basket to a poor boy like him.

There were bananas in the basket, so he emptied them on the floor before he took it. He thought about eating some of the bananas, but there were no ants on them and ants ate everything. Jamal was sure that his grandfather would share his food, and he would know what food was safe. He must know almost everything if all these people had been going to climb the mountain to see him. Jamal was pleased to have such a wise relation. He pushed the canister, with the ghost riddles painted on the side, into his basket and pulled the basket behind him. It was much heavier than he expected. He tried to balance it on his head like his cousins did, but the basket wobbled and he was afraid that the canister would fall out and roll back down the hill. He gave up and pulled the basket once more, bumping it over the stones and the people on the path. He took care not to actually tread on anyone, but it was hard to control the bag. When he started walking up the path he apologised to the aunties and uncles lying on the ground, but soon he had apologised so much to no one in particular, that he just pulled his basket over the people and walked as quickly as he could. He wanted to be away from this place.

He wanted to reach somewhere safe where he didn't have to keep deciding what to do. And he wanted someone else to do some thinking. He was sure that if only he could find his grandfather, he wouldn't have to keep on racking his brains. Grandfather would know how to stop the ghosts and how to make things normal again. He couldn't quite remember what his grandfather looked like – after all, he'd only seen him once before – but he remembered Grandfather's voice. It was loud and deep and chased away the witches that walked across the roofs at night. He was definitely the sort of man who would know what to do next.

How High is a Mountain?

The further Jamal walked, the fewer bodies he saw. *That's good,* he thought; *the ghosts don't like to climb.* This was the first thing he'd learnt about the ghosts. He decided to tell Grandfather, when he found him. In the meantime, he kept walking, dragging his basket up the steps.

The steps stopped suddenly, just as the path turned back on itself. Jamal stopped too. It was dark and he could hear the wild dogs at the bottom of the path, but everything was quiet around him. The ground was flat and rough – not solid rock like the steps, but gritty, like the roads near the market at home. There were buildings all around. Houses – white concrete houses with no doors or windows and vines growing through the walls. Jamal couldn't understand why these houses were empty. There were no bodies, no signs of ghosts, but no signs of people either. Strangely, Jamal felt more afraid here than he had at the bottom of the mountain, but it was dark and he was tired so he crept towards the closest house. He listened. There was no noise inside.

'Hello?'

He waited.

'Hello?'

Silence.

'Hello Auntie, Uncle, may I enter?'

He stepped inside. *Snap!* Jamal dropped his bag and jumped backwards, tripping as a black ... what? Something, he couldn't tell what! Then silence again. A moment later something flew past him. It brushed against his face and he screamed. Then again and again. Jamal was embarrassed – he had screamed like a parrot in a trap. They were bats, only bats that had been hiding inside the house.

Jamal wrinkled his nose - the smell was awful. The bats had lived here for a long time and the floor was covered in their droppings. But only three had left; where were the rest? Jamal had walked by the hollow trees where they roosted and he knew that this much poo meant a lot of bats. He moved to the next house. It was quieter, less smelly. He went inside, but not too far. Who knew what was hiding in this house.

Jamal stayed near the door. He untied the drinks from his back and leant against the wall. He would wait until it was light before he looked for his grandfather. The mountain was too big and too dangerous to climb in the dark. He drank one of the bottles of Fanta, then another, and another, until he felt sick. He threw an empty bottle outside. It smashed. Somehow the noise made Jamal feel less alone. A human noise in the silence. He burped, loudly, as loudly as he could. The noise echoed in the concrete room. *If I lived here,* Jamal thought, *I would drink Fanta and burp all the time.* Next minute he fell asleep, sliding down the wall and curling into a ball. He was still asleep when the bats returned to their roosts.

When he woke up he was hungry. But he had no food. If only he had known this would happen when he was at the bottom of the mountain, but he hadn't. He had another drink instead, though he was getting fed up with Fanta – he wanted a cool drink of water straight from a stream. The drinks he had were too sweet; they seemed to make him even thirstier. That was another thing to ask his grandfather. How can you feel even thirstier after you have had a drink? There were so many things that he'd never thought of before. He wondered if he would have known these things if he had been to school. His uncles had said that there was no point in sending him to school. That he was too stupid and too strange. He wondered if that was true. It probably was – after all, his uncles wouldn't have lied. Perhaps if he could find the ghosts and get them to leave him alone then he would be able to go to school. He decided not to tell anyone about wanting to go to school; he knew that even Grandfather would laugh if he shared this secret.

When Jamal left the house he looked around; he was at the edge of a village, or maybe a town, but an empty town. The houses had been built, but never lived in. This was the strangest of all the strange things that he had seen since he left home. Beyond the empty town the mountain rose up again, slowly at first then straight up like a wall. It was higher than it had seemed from the plain, and much steeper. He could see cracks and splits in the rock, but no paths. But there had to be a path – there was smoke rising from one of the cracks. Where there was smoke there were usually people. He went back to the house and collected his things. The drinks were much lighter now – there were only a few left. He was worried about carrying the cylinder up the mountain. The basket was almost worn through; if he kept dragging it there would soon be no basket at all. He decided to tie the cylinder, still wrapped in its basket, to his back. It was heavy, but he could manage, at least for a while. Jamal retied the blanket, picked up his book and headed across the deserted town, hoping to find a path when he got closer.

The path was there – not clear like the one that had led to the houses, but the ground had been walked on sometime in the past. The path rose steeply as soon as he left the last house behind and his feet slipped on the loose ground. Sometimes the path was not clear and Jamal sank to his knees in the soft soil, but when he found the path again he only sank to his ankles. It would be a hard climb. He looked at his feet, and where he was going to put his feet, but never far ahead. When he did look up, the slope seemed to go on forever, and beyond forever was the steep wall of rock that he was trying to reach. So he stopped looking up and looked down instead. If he thought about that rock he knew he'd give up, just stop walking, stay where he was and wait for the wild dogs to find him. It was just too high, too impossible. He felt as if he had been walking for days and now he knew he was about to fail. That's why he stopped looking and stopped thinking and just walked. He let one foot sink in the hot black grit then, before the grit covered his ankles he pulled out the other foot, only for it to sink again. He would have sat in the shade to rest, but there was no shade. He would have found a better path, but this was the only one, so he just kept walking.

The path twisted back on itself, creeping up the slope like a snake hiding from an eagle. He thought of the stories his mother had told him, before she left. The one about the giant snakes that guarded the mountain, or the one about the eagle that ate fish from the River of Life and was chased away by the water spirits. They were silly stories, told to make children laugh, and Jamal had liked to hear them, because back when his mother had told them he was only a child and he still knew how to laugh. Thinking about them now made him want to cry, but at least it stopped him thinking about what he would do if his grandfather was not on this mountain.

As the climb got steeper he saw a rope, as thick as his arm and covered in the dust and grit that had blown across the path. It was lying on the path in front of him. He thought it would be useful if he needed to sleep in a tree when the wild dogs came. But there were no trees here, so he hoped the dogs would stay away, but he tried to coil the rope – just in case. He couldn't. The rope was caught on something further up the mountain.

'Hey!' he shouted, the way he would have done if someone was holding the other end. He didn't really think anyone was there. There were no footprints, but he called anyway. It was good to hear a voice, even if it was only his own. No one answered. So Jamal followed the rope, coiling it up as he climbed. Pulling on the rope made the climb easier and the knots that were tied every few steps stopped his hands from slipping. It was a useful tool to help him climb the mountain, almost as useful as the steps had been. *It is a pity that I will have to take the rope with me,* he thought. *The next boy who climbs this mountain will not be as lucky as I am.*

Then he started to laugh. He had not thought of himself as lucky before. His uncles had told him that he was unlucky. His aunties had said that when he was born all the luck had left the family and his cousins had thrown stones at him when no one was looking, saying that he was cursed and trying to make him leave the compound. He had believed them all but now he was beginning to think that he was lucky. He had not died when the ghosts came, he had not died when he fell out of the tree, he had not even died of thirst on the journey across the sand, and he had found the icebox and all the bottles of Fanta. *Yes,* he thought to himself, *I am lucky, and I will find my grandfather and I will tell him how lucky I am.*

He reached the next bend in the path and saw that the rope was tied to a metal ring that was hammered into the rock. Jamal felt guilty. He should have left the rope where it was, ready for the next traveller. He threw the loops behind him, hoping that the rope would uncoil, but it didn't; it just tied itself in angry knots a couple of metres down the slope. *Yes,* he thought, *I am lucky - luckier than the next person who climbs this mountain — they will have a long walk before they reach that rope.*

Jamal turned back up the path and found the next rope, gave it a tug to make sure it was safe, and began climbing again. He laughed to himself, thinking how cross his uncle would have been if someone had rolled up the rope so he couldn't use it. Then he thought how very fortunate it was that his uncle wasn't here or he would surely have found a stick and beaten him.

It was while he was thinking about his uncle that he noticed two things. Firstly, he noticed that the air tasted different than it had done at the bottom of the mountain. It was sweeter on his tongue and lighter in his chest. It was clearer, too: he could see further, or at least he thought he could. But that couldn't be true. Air was air, the same for the birds as the lizards and the same for Jamal. He decided that he had just opened his eyes wider because there was more to see. This was something else that he would ask Grandfather about later. Then, as if to remind himself of how things ought to be, he heard sounds. Not just the flies that had come to lay their eggs at the bottom of the mountain, but proper daytime noises — insects and birds and all the scuttling and creeping sounds that belonged to the day. There was something else, a noise that Jamal had been waiting to hear. Someone was shouting, telling him to hurry up.

'Hey!' he shouted. 'Hey, where are you?'

'You're late. Do you think I live on air? Get a move on or you'll regret it.'

Jamal looked around, but he couldn't see where the voice was coming from. It was coming from the mountain, he was sure of that, but where on the mountain? The voice seemed to be everywhere, and whoever owned the voice seemed to be expecting him. They must have seen him walking up the path, maybe they had even seen him leaving the town, but Jamal couldn't see them. Were they hiding from him, or were they so small that they were hidden, or invisible like a witch? Or had he found the ghosts? Were they waiting for him, still hungry? Jamal stopped climbing, he needed to think.

It could be a witch, but Jamal didn't think it was. Witches were everywhere, Auntie Sheema had said so, but she had also said that they moved faster than a goat with its tail on fire. Jamal had never seen a goat with its tail on fire, but he had seen goats chased by a swarm of bees and they ran really fast, straight into the river. Jamal remembered laughing with his cousins, but that was before they said he was cursed. When he could still play with his cousins, when they would still play with him. No, the voice couldn't belong to a witch. A witch would not have called out; a witch would have run on the wind to find him. A witch would be here by now.

It could have been something very small, an animal spirit or the sort of devil that could hide in an eggshell, but Jamal didn't think it was. Such a small spirit would have a small voice and the voice he had heard was strong. Far away, but loud.

Jamal had heard that some mountains were alive – they were great spirits that protected the people who lived near them – but the voice wasn't deep enough to be a mountain. And, Jamal thought, this mountain could not have a spirit living in it because it had not protected the people who had waited at the bottom.

He was left with two choices: he had found where the ghosts lived, or there was a man hiding in the mountain, a man who had found the way to make his voice echo where there were no walls. If he had found the ghosts, then what did they want with him? He had no soul, they could not eat him. That meant that when he reached them they would still be hungry. Did he want to meet angry ghosts? Would they let him escape? Would they tell him what they wanted? He wasn't sure. It could also be a man, a man who had lit a fire and who had found a way to make his voice loud, like the voices on the radio. Jamal needed to know; he needed to be prepared before he followed the voice.

'Smoke,' he said. 'I need to see the smoke.' He got up and looked up at the mountain again.

'Why did you stop, stupid boy?' shouted the voice. 'Get up here now. I told you I was hungry.'

Jamal stared up at the cracks in the mountain, trying to remember where the smoke had been. He found it, almost straight ahead but not quite. It was grey, definitely grey, not yellow like the ghost smoke. There was a man hiding in the mountain. A man who was alive, like Jamal. He grabbed the rope and started climbing – almost running, if you counted pulling yourself up a steep slope covered with slippery gravel and loose stones as running. He reached the end of the rope and the end of the slope. There was a narrow strip of flat ground before the vertical rock rose in front of him.

He could see that people had been there before, lots of people. They had brought things and left things. Warnings and offerings and rubbish, so much rubbish. If this was where his grandfather lived then his grandfather was not a tidy person. Jamal was a tidy person. He swept his hut every day – he swept outside as well – and he washed his clothes and his blankets.

He was not clean now – he had walked too much and had too little water – but usually he was clean. He didn't like being dirty; his skin itched and his eyes were sore. He hoped that he would get a chance to wash himself soon. He looked at the rubbish and the flags and the offerings, trying to work out where the man was hiding.

The Old Man in the Cave

He smelt the fire and walked towards the smell till he could see the flames. Soon he could see an old man sitting, almost naked, next to the fire. As he got closer there was another smell. It was disgusting – it made his stomach turn. He hoped the smell didn't come from the old man, but it did. He wanted to find his grandfather but he wasn't sure if he wanted to be related to this strange, smelly old man. He wondered what to say. He hadn't seen his grandfather since his mother had died, and that was a long time ago. How could he be sure that this was his grandfather and how should he ask without sounding disrespectful? He was still thinking what to say when the old man spoke.

'Where have you been?' His voice was deep, almost deep enough to make the rocks shake. 'You took your time. I watched, you kept stopping. Didn't you hear me call?'

'I'm sorry.' Jamal could hear that his voice sounded like a mouse squeaking in a thunderstorm. 'I tried to come quickly. I think you are my grandfather.'

'Do you now? And why is that? Do you know how many wives I've had, how many children? I don't even know how many grandchildren there might be. How should I know if you are one of them? I don't think you are, you're not strong like me. What have you brought?'

Jamal had no gift. He had not thought to bring anything from home, he'd only thought about getting away, and about the ghosts. He couldn't stop thinking about the ghosts; he was still thinking about them.

'I'm sorry, Grandfather, my gift is very small, only these drinks.'

The old man, who might have been Jamal's grandfather, snatched the bottles. He drank one straight away, then threw the empty bottle so that it joined the piles of rubbish that Jamal had seen earlier. Then the old man opened the second bottle, drinking that the same way. He held up the last bottle.

'Are you thirsty?' the old man asked.

Jamal thought he was offering to share the last drink, but he was not that sort of grandfather.

41

'If you are, you can get yourself a drink of water – there is half a bottle in the cave. Put this next to the water. I'll drink it later.'

Jamal took the bottle – it was Sprite. He had only taken two bottles of Sprite from the ice box and he had been saving this one. Reluctantly he headed for the cave. It was cooler there, but too dark, after the daylight outside. He paused by the entrance, letting his eyes get used to the blackness. It was good that he did: there were three – no, four – uneven steps that led to the main part of the cave. Jamal saw where the old man slept and where he kept his clothes. He saw rows of pots and boxes and bottles that smelt even worse than the old man did. Jamal didn't go too close; he imagined what they might contain – dead snakes and monkey bones and … no, he didn't want to think what else might be there. He saw the water bottle, next to a bowl of dried-up stew that had been kept for too long. Jamal put the Sprite next to the bowl and picked up the water. It did not look fresh either, but Jamal was from the country and he knew water was not always fresh, so he tipped the bottle up.

'Ugh!' He spat it out. Jamal wasn't even sure it *was* water; it burnt his mouth and made his eyes run.

'Good, eh?' The old man slapped him on the back. 'Now don't waste it, boy, you won't get water like that at home.' The old man laughed. 'Now bring the bowl. Let's eat.'

Jamal put the bottle down and picked up the bowl of what he thought was last week's lunch then followed the old man back out to the fire.

'So now we fill our bellies. What else have you got in there? Tinned meat; fresh? Or this year's yams ready to roast?'

There were flies buzzing around the stew and Jamal shooed them away.

'They're back then. I wished them away and they went. Now you've brought them back. Not very clever, are you, boy? Bringing the flies back to the mountain.'

Jamal said nothing; he wasn't ready to ask about the ghosts yet. Ask why they had come and why they went away and what that had to do with the flies. So he just nodded.

'Now, boy, why do you think I'm your grandfather?' The old man poked at the fire, adding logs ready for the yams that he thought were in Jamal's bag. 'Who was your father? Your mother? Where are you from?'

Jamal tried to answer his questions, but he didn't know his father and he wasn't sure of the name of the town that was near the compound. But he told the old man what he could and he described his journey – not the people, just the places. He didn't feel like talking about the people.

'Could be,' the old man said, chewing some betel. 'There was a girl called Asha, I think. It's hard to remember the girls, you know. Too many of them.' He spat out the remains of the nut. The red spittle hit the bowl then hissed in the fire as it fell in a sticky blob into the flames. 'My third wife, Nnedi, she had a girl. I think she was called Asha. You said I went to the funeral - when was that?'

'About three years ago, maybe four. I was only small,' Jamal said.

'You're still small, boy, still small, but you're right, you could be my grandson.' The old man slapped Jamal on the back again. 'What did you say your name was? Jamal? Strange name, not one I recognise. Why did your mother give you that name? What does it mean? Runt of the litter, I think.'

The old man started to cough.

'Something to do with the flies,' his grandfather said. 'The cough came when the flies left. It'll go soon, now the flies are back.'

Jamal couldn't understand why his grandfather said that. It was a bad cough, the sort of cough that comes before dying, not the sort of cough that was caused by flies.

Jamal did not want to see any more dying, so he turned away and walked back to the cave.

When he returned his grandfather had stopped coughing. He was looking in Jamal's basket, the one that was tied inside the cloth. He did not look happy.

'What's this?' He was pointing at the cylinder, then he looked at Jamal and kicked the cylinder away.

'What good is that to an old man with an empty belly?'

Jamal started to explain, but his grandfather wasn't listening.

'What's wrong with you? Do you think we can eat this, this poison? You come up here, talking of children and grandchildren, bringing no gifts, no food, only poison. Are you trying to kill me?'

Jamal was confused; he hadn't expected his grandfather to be like this. He thought his grandfather would give him breakfast and warm tea and tell him why the ghosts had come.

'I did not come to kill you. You are my grandfather. I am your daughter's son, you said so. I came for your help. Why would I come all this way to poison you?'

'How can I help you when my belly's empty? If there is no food for me, there is none for you either, boy. Don't think I will give you any of this. That is not hospitality. Sharing food, that is hospitality. But you, you come here expecting food when you bring nothing. Tell me, boy, what else have you got hidden there? There is something else, I can see it.'

Jamal shook his head, afraid he might say the wrong thing and make his grandfather shout again. This was not the sort of grandfather he was hoping to find.

His grandfather stirred the pot of stew on the fire. Jamal was hungry, but the stew smelt bad, and he was sure that some of the old man's spit had landed in it earlier.

'There's none for you, so don't look hungry.' His grandfather added half of the bottle of water to the bowl. 'Yes, you could be Asha's boy – you are ugly like her, and ungrateful. Well, I was pleased when she left and I'll be pleased when you leave. So just show me what else you've got there and get on your way.'

Why was this old man so rude? Jamal was sure that he hadn't done anything wrong. He had given his grandfather the last of his drinks – it wasn't his fault that he didn't have any food. And as for being ugly, was that a reason to be cross? Jamal couldn't help being ugly, and in any case, he didn't think he was ugly – dirty, yes, but not ugly. And his grandfather did not appear to mind people being dirty. Jamal thought that his grandfather had never washed in his life. He didn't like Grandfather saying that his mum was ugly either. She wasn't. Jamal sometimes forgot the shape of her hands or the sound of her voice, but he was sure she was not ugly.

'So, ugly boy, what's going on out there? Where is everybody? Why haven't they brought my lunch?'

Jamal tried to explain about the ghosts and the smell and his family dying and all the animals being dead and people at the bottom of the mountain and why he had brought the red canister with the pictures but the old man didn't listen.

'So you expect me to believe all that, do you? Then tell me this, what makes you think I will help you? Especially when you haven't brought my breakfast?'

Jamal couldn't understand why his grandfather was so bothered about his stomach when so many people were dead. Jamal fetched the cylinder from where it had landed.

'Please, Grandfather,' he said, 'please tell me what it says. Read the stories to me.'

'Bad magic. New magic. Not the sort of magic I want anything to do with. Throw it away.' The old man kicked the cylinder into the fire. Jamal tried to pull it out but the metal was too hot and choking smoke began to swirl, wrapping around the picture of the fish in the net and the tree without leaves.

'I told you. Bad magic,' his grandfather said before starting to cough again.

Jamal started to explain how he used to keep the spirits away from his family and how, when the ghosts came, he'd failed. He explained that he wanted to put things right, to make the spirits happy but he didn't know how, but how he was sure that the pictures on the cylinder were important.

The more he said, the angrier his grandfather became.

'What spirits, ugly boy?' the old man asked. 'Do you get money to drive the spirits away? Do you get food? Why didn't you stay where you were? Why didn't you stay away from me?' He hit Jamal on the head, making his ears sting.

His grandfather was asking so many questions. Jamal's head began to spin and the scent of nutmeg slipped into his nostrils. For once he wasn't afraid; his grandfather was there and he would watch him while the spirits came.

'Get up, get up, lazy. Get off my mountain.'

Jamal felt a sharp pain in his ribs as the old man kicked him.

'I said, go.'

He didn't understand. Why was Grandfather kicking him? What had he done wrong? He got up; he was still shaking and wanted to stay on the ground but the old man had sharp toes and Jamal wanted to get out of his way. He stumbled and reached for his grandfather's arm to steady himself.

'Get away, boy! I don't want you here. This place is mine, find your own living. Find it somewhere else, a long way from here.' The old man flung the cylinder, still hot from the fire. It caught Jamal on the arm, knocking him over. As Jamal stumbled, his book fell from under his blanket. He scrambled to save it, but he was too late. The old man had seen the book and started screaming at Jamal. If Jamal thought he was cross before it was nothing to how cross he was when he saw the book. It was only a book but Grandfather seemed to be afraid of it. He was shouting strange, mixed-up words. Some words that Jamal understood and some that he didn't. All shouted in a voice that sounded like a pack of wild dogs. Then the mad old man threw stones at Jamal and Jamal decided to run.

'Good! Go away! Get out of here. Take that book with you. No wonder everyone has died. Do you know nothing? Bringing a thing like that here, to my mountain. This is a place for the old gods, not the new. This is the Mountain Without God. Keep that book of gods away from me. No wonder the flies have returned. Get away and take that book with you. Get off my mountain!'

Jamal ran. Grandfather threw stones and cursed Jamal until he was out of sight, then he turned back to his fire, still mumbling about a book and the mountain and the gods.

Jamal didn't stick to the path. He ran and slipped and fell straight down the mountain, away from the old man and into the safety of the trees. He didn't stop until his heart was pounding in his chest and his feet were cut by the stones and thorns he'd slid across. His legs collapsed and he sat on the ground taking great gulps of air, trying to make up for the breaths he hadn't taken when he was running.

A great cloud of yellow butterflies rose into the air, then settled back down, almost exactly where they'd been. Jamal had never seen so many butterflies together and he had never seen them fly without opening their wings. He reached out to touch one. Then he stopped. They were all dead. The ground was covered with thousands and thousands of dead butterflies. He had thought that the earth was soft with a carpet of leaves, but it wasn't. The ground felt soft because he was sitting on a cushion stuffed with the bodies of yellow butterflies.

He looked at his hands; they were grey with the dust from the wings of the butterflies, and they shone where the sun caught the scales sticking to his hands. Suddenly Jamal wanted to cry. The ghosts must have been there, killing every butterfly in the world. But why? Butterflies had such tiny souls – they held the souls of babies who had been born dead. What could the ghosts want with them? Jamal knew that he couldn't stay there. He walked slowly until he left the last of the butterflies behind, wiping his hands as he walked. He tried to wipe the scales away, but he couldn't. They stuck to his skin and his clothes so he couldn't forget.

When he was sure he had left the last of the butterflies behind, he walked out of the trees and kept walking until he came to a red dust road. Then he curled in a ball and pulled his blanket over him and slept.

A Place to Rest

'Here's another one. Bring a bag.'

The woman's voice, loud and exhausted, cut into Jamal's dream. Or maybe it didn't; maybe the voice was part of the dream. He hadn't seen any women since he had stolen the drinks from the drink seller. He was sure that this was just another dream, until he felt his hair pulled upwards.

'Ahh!' he shouted.

The person let go of his hair and Jamal's head hit the ground with a thump.

'Ahhh!' he said again.

'This one's alive. Bring a stretcher … and the oxygen. Quick!'

The woman with the tired voice suddenly sounded wide awake. She was stroking his head, touching his cheeks. Jamal wanted to get up. He wanted to tell her to go away. Tell her that no one came close to him, that the spirits would notice if she touched him. But he didn't say anything, he just looked up at her while his head spun and his stomach churned.

'It's all right, sweetie, you'll be OK now.'

Jamal couldn't understand what was wrong with this strange woman. What would be all right and who was sweetie?

'Hurry up, will you? God knows how he survived but we're not going to lose him now. Come on!'

Jamal was about to ask what was happening but people were all around him. Everyone was touching him and he wanted to make them stop but there were too many people. Something was put on his face; it made his mouth and nose cold. Jamal thought they were trying to stop him breathing and pushed them away, but the woman with the tired voice held his hands.

'Don't worry, sweetie. Don't fight. We're here to help you.'

She was talking about sweetie again. *Maybe she thinks I look like her friend,* thought Jamal. Or was she called Sweetie and she was telling him not to bother her? It was all so confusing. They had put Jamal on a narrow bed and they were carrying him somewhere. He couldn't work out where because so many people were walking around him and leaning over him. All talking at once.

There was another bump as they put his bed down. Jamal tried to push the people away again. He knew he'd been right; they were blowing spirits into his mouth – he could smell the nutmeg on his face. The last thing he heard was the tired woman sounding very worried.

'He's having a fit. Put your foot down; let's get out of here.'

The spirits came and went and Jamal felt confused. When he woke up he was lying on a mattress, but the floor must have been damp because the mattress was high above it. They had put a plastic sheet above the mattress as well. It fell like a tent over Jamal, but it kept him dry so he didn't complain. It was strange, though, because the people who were outside the tent didn't look wet and they didn't wear coats or hats. The people outside the tent were very nice to him. They smiled and told him to rest. Jamal was happy to just rest because he had walked further than he'd ever walked before.

Sometimes they put their hands under the tent and wiped him with cold cloths. Sometimes they put a small stick in his mouth and told him not to bite it. He thought that strange. Only babies bite sticks and he wasn't a baby. They brought him food and water to drink and sometimes a very small drink in a very small cup. He didn't like the small drink – it made him very sleepy – but he liked the other things they brought him so he took the small drink when they gave it to him and he didn't complain.

After a while the people outside the tent took the tent away and said that he didn't need it any more. They didn't put the mattress back on the floor, though, and when they told Jamal that he should try to walk he was surprised to find that the floor was not wet at all. He asked for his blanket but the people from outside the tent said it was lost. Jamal felt sad but the people were so nice he didn't tell them he was sad.

The woman with the tired voice came to visit him and gave him a gift wrapped up in a red cloth.

She smiled when he opened it and found his book inside.

'I rescued it,' she said. 'I should have had it destroyed, but I checked it out and it's OK.'

Jamal didn't know why the book should have been destroyed; it had such pretty patterns inside.

'Please don't tell anyone that it's the same book. I'll get in trouble if you do.'

Jamal wasn't sure why she would get in trouble for returning his book but he thought she was nice and he didn't want her to get into trouble, so he didn't mention his book to anyone.

He was given clean clothes to wear and milk to drink and three meals every day. He noticed that his arms were getting fatter and he felt strong. All the people who talked to him were nice and no one called him names or pushed him or hit him with sticks. This was a good place to rest and sometimes he even forgot about the smell of the ghosts and the fact that his grandfather didn't want to see him and that all his uncles and aunties were dead.

One day, when he was sitting outside, trying to forget about all the people who had died and trying to make stories from the patterns in his book, a soldier told him to follow her to the office. Jamal wanted to ask someone if this would be all right but no one was there but the soldier. He closed his book and followed her across the compound. She told him that he must tell the judge what had happened and that it was important for him to tell the truth.

'Why would I lie?' Jamal asked. The soldier smiled and rubbed Jamal's head.

'I don't know, sweetie.'

Who was this Sweetie? And why did everyone mix him up with Jamal?

'I am sure a boy like you wouldn't have any reason to lie.' The soldier smiled at him again and opened the door to the office. 'Now just remember, sweetie, tell the truth.'

The judge sat at a desk and another soldier sat next to him, and another sat in the corner tapping his fingers quietly on a machine that was sort of like a typewriter and sort of like a light. Jamal wanted to look at the machine but the soldier guided him to a seat opposite the judge.

'Now, young man, you mustn't be afraid.'

Jamal wasn't sure what he should be afraid *of* – this room was much less frightening than most of the things he had seen and the judge was much less frightening than his grandfather. But after the judge mentioned being afraid, Jamal began to think about all the things that could be frightening and felt very afraid indeed.

'That's good. I am going to ask you some questions and we are going to write down what you say on the computer over there. Do you understand?'

Jamal didn't understand the bit about the computer but he understood the rest so he said yes.

'It's Jamal, isn't it?'

Jamal nodded

'An unusual name, where does it come from?'

'My mother gave it to me.'

'Ah yes, but why did she give you that name? What part of the country is the name from? What tribe?'

Jamal didn't know. He didn't think he was from a tribe. He thought he was from a family. He explained this to the judge. He was surprised that he had to explain about families to this man. He looked clever, he looked as if he had been to school, but he didn't seem to know about families.

'Never mind,' the judge said. 'Let's move on. Did you see who threw the gas?'

Jamal didn't know what the judge was talking about, so he shook his head.

'Well, did you see anyone near your village? Anyone who didn't belong there?'

Jamal still didn't know what the judge was talking about so he shook his head again. He thought about telling the judge about the men in the Jeep, but he hadn't really seen them, just heard their voices, and as the judge didn't seem to be very bright Jamal didn't say anything.

'We're not making much progress here, are we? Can you tell us how you survived the gas attack?'

Jamal felt better about this; he didn't know what a gas attack was but he remembered the lessons that the Imam had given him.

'Because it was Allah's will, sir,' Jamal said.

He was very pleased that he had been able to answer one of the questions.

'Oh dear, let's try again. Why were you on the mountain?'

Another easy question. Jamal was getting the hang of this at last.

'I was visiting my grandfather.'

'And why didn't you stay with your grandfather?'

'Because he told me to go away, sir. He kicked me and threw things at me and told me to get off the mountain, sir. I don't think he remembered me, sir. He didn't want to see me at all. So I went away before he kicked me again.'

'And is your grandfather still alive?'

'Yes, sir. I think so, sir. I told you he kicked me, sir, and threw things at me. He was alive when he told me to go away, sir. But he had a bad cough, sir, so I think he might be very sick.'

'And your grandfather lives on the mountain? How strange. I thought no one would go near that place. Don't the locals think it's haunted?'

Jamal nodded. 'I don't know if it is haunted, sir, but my grandfather lives there, in a cave. I don't know why he doesn't live in the empty houses, sir – they are much more comfortable – but he lives in a cave, sir, high on the mountain.'

'Send someone up there to trace him, will you, sergeant?'

Jamal imagined how angry his grandfather would be if they brought him off the mountain and decided that he would have to find somewhere else to live. Grandfather would definitely blame him if the soldiers brought him off the mountain and Jamal didn't want to get kicked again.

'And you really can't tell us anything else?'

Jamal shook his head once again.

'OK, sergeant. I think we're finished here. See if you can arrange a school or an orphanage or something until his grandfather collects him.'

The judge looked down at his papers.

'Clearly the boy's a fool, no point wasting any time with him.'

Jamal knew he wasn't a fool; he hadn't been to school but he wasn't a fool. He was about to tell the judge but the soldier pushed him towards the door.

'He is definitely a fool, your honour. The medics have said that he's simple. They don't know if it was the gas or if he's always been that way, but they think it was probably the gas attack.'

Jamal wondered why the soldier was being so mean, when she had been so nice before. He might have asked her, but she kept pushing him towards the door.

'Yes, sergeant, a sad case. Take him back where you found him, will you? We have other interviews today.'

That was it. They had finished with Jamal and now wanted to send him to live with his grandfather.

'Why did you say I was simple?' Jamal asked when they got outside. 'I'm not simple, and I'm not a fool.'

'I know you're not,' said the soldier, 'but it's better the judge thinks you are. When they saw your Qur'an, they thought you were one of the terrorists. I didn't want them to send you to jail. If they think you are too stupid to be a terrorist and too simple to tell them about the terrorists, they won't bother with you.'

Jamal wondered if terrorists were one of the mountain tribes that the judge had asked about. He'd never heard of them but the judge seemed to think there were lots of tribes and that they were very important. He was about to ask the soldier why it was best not to be a terrorist when they reached the cooks with their big pot of groundnut stew.

'Well done,' said the soldier. 'I bet you're looking forward to going home and eating your mother's stew instead of this.'

Jamal smiled at her and nodded his head. He knew he couldn't go home and he knew he wouldn't go with his grandfather. The only thing he didn't know was where he *would* be going.

Soup

The soldier turned away and left Jamal with the cooks. The food smelt good – the food always smelt good – but it wasn't like his auntie's food. The chilli prickled his nose, but somehow it prickled it in a different way from Auntie's chillies. There was fish in the stew, but it wasn't the same fish as Auntie used; it wasn't the fish Mr Onuzo caught in the river. *Yes*, thought Jamal, *the food is good but it's not right* – and because Auntie was dead, food would never be quite right again. He decided that maybe he would miss lunch today. He would not have to go hungry – there was always something to be had if you knew where to be and who to ask – but first he wanted to spend some time thinking about home.

'Hey, boy,' the cook called to him. 'Looks to me like you were about to be somewhere else. Don't you like my stew?'

'Yes, sir, it's good stew, sir. It's just ...' Jamal didn't know what to say.

'It's just not your mama's stew, hey?'

'Not Auntie's stew, sir. My mama died when I was little, but my auntie makes good stew.' Jamal thought about the smell when Auntie fell on the fire. '*Made good stew, she made good stew, sir, and soup. Her soup was the best thing she made. It was ...*' Jamal didn't know how to tell the cook about Auntie's soup.

The cook smiled as if he knew exactly how Auntie's soup tasted. 'Hmm, it takes good soil to make good soup and the soil you grew in is always the best.'

The cook called the kitchen boy over. 'You keep stirring that pot. If it burns I'll beat you.' The kitchen boy's eyes widened. Jamal guessed that, nice as the cook seemed, he'd beaten the boy before. Then, after slapping the kitchen boy's head, just to remind him what might be in store, he called Jamal to the back of the kitchen.

'Now, young man, let's see if we can make soup like your auntie made you, shall we?' The cook took a small pot from the shelf and added chicken stock, two spoons of cooked tomatoes and some chopped onions.

'So, we have the base, now we need to make it taste like home.' The cook took a plate and put little piles of spices on it until it looked like a red and yellow map of the mountains. Then he poured out a cup of water and gave it to Jamal. 'This is what you do,' he said. 'You dip your finger in the spice, then taste it. Like this.' He touched the top of the reddest pile of spice with his little finger, then sucked the spice till his finger was clean. Jamal could see the cook's eyes beginning to water.

'Then you tell me if ...' The cook's voice had gone quiet and slightly squeaky. He coughed. 'If you remember that spice in your auntie's soup. And don't take too much, you understand? These spices are hot.'

Jamal nodded and carefully tried the first pile of spice. He left the one that had made the cook cough and started with one that was bright yellow. It was soft as the dust that covered moth wings. It wasn't hot like chillies, but it still made his tongue sting. It was bitter, like the mixture that the health worker gave him to kill worms, almost like the taste of ants when you crunched them between your teeth. It wasn't a bad taste, but it wasn't the right taste for soup. He shook his head.

'Have a drink then try another.'

Jamal did, trying one spice after another, eventually selecting five different spices that reminded him of auntie's soup.

'Good,' said the cook. 'Now some bitter leaves. Try these. Should we add these? Or these ones?'

And so Jamal and the cook spent the rest of the morning making soup. They stopped when the soldiers came for their lunch. Began again when the cook and the kitchen boys had their rice and stew. Jamal did not have any stew; he wanted to wait for the soup. But he did have a bowl of rice, and a small plate of fried plantain, just to keep him going till the soup was ready.

After lunch and after the cook had told everyone else what to do, they went back to the soup. It had been cooking slowly while they had been eating and Jamal thought that it tasted better, but still not right. Eventually Jamal said that the soup tasted just like Auntie's. It didn't, not really, but it nearly did. The cook told Jamal that he wouldn't be able to match Auntie's soup perfectly because he didn't have her cooking pot. Jamal thought he was just making excuses but he didn't say anything. He didn't think that would have been fair, not when the cook had tried so hard to make him food from home.

Jamal sat under a tree, the one where the lizards hid in the bark. The soup was good, almost as good as Auntie's. It still didn't taste of the river fish but Jamal had to admit that it was very good. He put down his spoon and wiped the inside of his bowl with his finger - he didn't want to waste even the tiniest amount. Then he put down the bowl and started to cry.

Learning from a Fish?

Jamal left his bowl under the tree and headed for his room. Usually he wouldn't have dared to leave his bowl in the compound but he guessed the cook might forgive him this once. *And if he doesn't forgive me, I don't care,* Jamal thought. *Even if he shouts and screams and hits me like he hit the kitchen boy. Because even if he does he still won't be as frightening as Grandfather.* Jamal threw a stone at a lizard. He missed.

'I wasn't even aiming at you,' he said. 'I was just throwing the stone and you happened to be there.' He couldn't even manage to be mean when he wanted to. Jamal needed to find somewhere to think. He went up to his room and looked around. No one was watching. He slipped inside and took his book from the top of the little cupboard where he kept his things – clean shorts, some pencils and one of the small black pebbles from the mountain. He squeezed himself under the bed and realised he must have grown since he'd been on the base. When he arrived he could hide under the bed easily, but it was difficult now. *If I stay at this place much longer,* he thought, *I'll have to find somewhere else to hide.*

He opened his book and touched the patterns with his finger. He realised that the patterns kept repeating. When he first got the book, he thought that every pattern and every page was different, but as he'd started to look more carefully he could see this wasn't true. On some pages he could find the same pattern again and again. There was one that looked like a monkey in a tree, its tail hanging down below the branch, and there was a butterfly, sometimes with its wings open, sometimes closed. That picture was only on a few of the pages. The book had fallen open on his favourite page. It had a fish jumping out of a stream. Sometimes the fish was trying to catch a fly, sometimes it wasn't, but it was the same fish and the same stream.

He heard footsteps and looked out. He could see a pair of feet. He knew if he kept quiet the feet would go away. People never thought to look down – they were adults, they didn't know about hiding under beds. The feet walked away from the bed and Jamal went back to his book. He wanted to look at the patterns again. He was sure they must mean something, tell some kind of story, if only he could work it out. He decided to start with the fish. He turned the pages until he found a pattern where the fish was near the edge of the page, then he followed it across the page and back again. Jamal liked this fish, it was definitely the best of the animals in the book. The fish was always trying to get the fly even though he never quite reached it. *Maybe this fish is like a boy,* Jamal thought. *Maybe it's like a boy who wants to find ghosts and who keeps going even though people keep stopping him.*

'You are talking rubbish, Jamal,' he said out loud. 'It's just a pattern, it doesn't mean anything. The judge was right: you *are* simple.' He shut the book as hard as he could and punched the bed frame above him – and then he found out he wasn't alone.

'Ow!'

The woman with the tired voice leant down and peered under the bed. She frowned at Jamal.

'Oh, I thought you'd gone. I mean, I didn't know,' Jamal said.

'Good, because I wouldn't like to think that you meant to punch me.'

Jamal wondered if he should explain that he wouldn't ever have punched her on purpose but he wasn't quite sure if she was serious. She got off the bed and knelt down, looking right at him.

'You're not simple, Jamal. Don't listen to anyone who tells you that you are. You have been sick. You might always be sick or you might get better, but you are not simple. You should go to school if you can and then you can learn to read your book and understand the stories.'

She smiled. 'How about coming out from under the bed?'

Jamal was surprised that someone who looked so tired would say such nice things to him. When his aunties were tired they would shout at his cousins and shout at Jamal. Sometimes they would even shout at his uncles, but his uncles shouted back. Sometimes they even sat by Jamal's hut and drank palm wine and then made Jamal promise that he wouldn't tell. He wasn't sure why. All the men Jamal knew drank palm wine and they all pretended they didn't, especially on the days when the Imam came to visit. But it was too late now. He couldn't ask them why it was a secret when everyone knew. The woman with the tired voice and the tired face hadn't shouted at him, she had told him to go to school. He made up his mind to think about what she said. But going to school would have to wait. He had important plans to make and not much time to make them.

Jamal was sure that his grandfather would not come down the mountain to fetch him. But the soldiers would go and find his grandfather. He was sure about that because the soldiers all seemed to be afraid of the judge. Next he tried to count the days in his head. It would take a day to get to the mountain and a day to get back. He didn't think that the soldiers would try very hard to find his grandfather but he thought that they might pretend to look. Maybe they would find somewhere to stay for a few days or maybe they would go home to their mothers while they could. He was sure it would be at least a week and probably more, before they came back to say that Jamal was alone. But what if they found Grandfather? What if Grandfather was afraid of the soldiers? What if, instead of hiding in the cave or throwing rocks, he came here with the soldiers? What if Jamal had to go back with him? No, no, no, Jamal didn't want that; he had to find the ghosts and that meant leaving here and finding where they lived.

And what if the soldiers couldn't find his grandfather? What had the judge said? Something about sending Jamal to 'Anof-anage'. He hadn't heard of that place. It might be very far away: how would he find the ghosts if he was sent away again? He decided to ask the cook where it was. The cook was clearly very clever. He managed to feed everyone and always have food left over to sell at the gate. Yes, Jamal thought, the cook would know where Anof-anage was.

The judge said they would send him there while he was waiting. Would they do that today or tomorrow? How soon? He ran after the woman with the sad voice. He would ask her. Did he have one day, or two, or even three?

There had been other children in the compound when he first arrived but they had already gone. Jamal thought they had been sent to a kind of jail. From what he had found out by listening to the cooks and the cleaners it was a special jail for children, where the guards were very strict mamas instead of policemen. He wondered if he would be sent there. Jamal was sure that some of the cooks made up stories so maybe they were making up stories about the jail, but, just in case, he had to get away before they locked him up with the other children.

He went outside, but the woman with the sad voice had gone. He picked up a stick and started making shapes in the dust. The shapes could have been anything, or they could have been a list of things that he wanted to find – a bag, a bottle, some coins, or was it some *akara* and a ball – or maybe a pile of dough balls? As he thought, the shapes became less like pictures and more like squiggles. Then the squiggles turned into patterns and the patterns turned into the marks from his book.

He was looking at the patterns when the soldier came back to talk to him.

'That's good,' she said. 'You should keep practising. You'll be writing soon, especially if you pay attention when you go to school.'

Jamal looked up from his drawing; he thought she had come to tell him that he had to leave.

'Don't look so worried, Jamal. I only came to tell you that a patrol has been sent out to find your grandfather, but we haven't found a place to send you yet. You will have to stay here until Friday.'

Jamal grinned. Friday was good. Friday meant he had almost a week to get ready.

'See, you have three more days to enjoy Cook's stew. Now run and play.'

Jamal ran to where the cooks were making supper; there was no one to play with but he was always welcome in the kitchen. He heard the soldier laughing. He wondered if he looked silly when he ran. Why else would she laugh at him? Jamal thought.

He helped the kitchen boy to peel the vegetables then they threw stones at cans till supper was ready to be served. When he had eaten his supper, he slipped through the tables and went up to the old cook. He was drinking tea and chewing something – not betel, his teeth weren't red - but something. The cook spat it out. Yuk!

'You want Afiba? He's cleaning up. You can help him if you want, but don't stop him working or you'll both feel the back of my hand.'

So that was the kitchen boy's name. Jamal had never heard him called anything but 'boy'. Jamal hadn't called him that – it seemed too rude. He'd just say 'Hi' and Afiba said the same thing back. But it was nice to know his name. *Not much use now though,* thought Jamal. *Not now I'm going away.*

'No, sir. I was looking for you,' Jamal said. 'I get so hungry in the night. Is there anything left from supper?'

The cook lifted his hand and Jamal flinched away from the blow, but instead of hitting his ear the cook put his hand under Jamal's chin and shook his head.

'Growing at last, eh? I can remember being a boy, you know. I was always hungry too. I tell you what, I've got a few bean cakes left. I'll wrap them in newspaper and you can hide them in your locker.'

Jamal thanked the cook and tucked his prize under his arm.

'Now don't go getting grease on the sheets or we'll both get in trouble, eh?'

Jamal didn't expect it to be so easy. He opened the parcel, just to check: there were six delicious bean cakes inside. *I'll just have one,* thought Jamal, *while they're hot.* It was perfect. Hot and crispy on the outside, while the bean curd was soft and spicy. Grease ran down his fingers as he ate. *Maybe just one more,* he said to himself. *After all, they're not so good cold and they are very good hot.*

He ran back to his room to hide the food. When he pushed the package into the cupboard the paper caught on the door. A bean cake escaped from the parcel and fell right into Jamal's hand.

'Guess I'd better eat it now,' he said, before pushing the rest into the cupboard, right at the back where no one would see them.

Jamal then went outside to work out how he'd get the other things he needed. But he was shooed back into his room.

'Too late for playing,' said the nurse. 'Bed for you, young man.' There was no arguing with this nurse. So Jamal went back inside and got ready for bed.

The First Plan

J amal didn't go to sleep, not straight away. He needed to plan what to do next. He didn't want to run away with nothing – he remembered how hungry he had been when he set off to find his grandfather. He needed to think about where to go as well. He had been following the tracks that the ghosts had left, but the soldiers had brought him here in a truck. The ghosts could be anywhere. How was he going to find them again? He pulled at the cord of his pyjamas; it was a good long piece of string so he could make a list of what he needed to do.

Find out where Anof-anage was. He tied a knot in the string.

Get some food for the journey. He tied another knot.

Find out if anyone else has seen the ghosts. Yet another knot went on the string.

All this thinking was making him hungry. Jamal leant over and took the last of the bean cakes from his cupboard. He was sure that filling his belly would help him to think. He ate the cakes, licking his fingers when he finished to make sure that none was wasted. At last he went back to his list.

Get some drinks for the journey. Knot.

Get a bag, a good strong one, to carry my stuff. Knot, knot.

Steal a blanket and some spare clothes. Knot, knot.

He would have to stop adding to the list as there was not much string left. Just enough to keep his pyjamas from falling down. There was one more thing he needed to do.

Check if the compound door is locked at night.

He didn't tie a knot for that. Instead, he slipped out of bed, trying not to make any noise as he walked across the room. He opened the door and the screen door silently. He closed the first door but the screen door slammed shut. Jamal had forgotten about the big spring that shut it tight. He froze, expecting someone to call out. But no one noticed – except one of the colonel's dogs, and the dogs were always barking at something.

Jamal started towards the kitchens, wondering if he might find a small snack or two while he was there.

The frogs were calling as he reached the kitchen and moths were bouncing off the kerosene lamps. He'd have to be back in his bed soon, before the nurse came round to check he was asleep. But he thought he might just have time to see the cook, if he was quick.

The kitchen was dark except for one small light in the corner. Jamal looked around; there was no sign of the cook. Jamal guessed that the cook had forgotten about the light and he went to turn it off. He remembered when his auntie's hut had caught fire. They had tried to put it out – they had even let Jamal help, carrying water to the edge of the compound – but it was no use, the hut burnt right down and Auntie Asmel had to share a hut with Auntie Terese. Neither auntie was very happy until a new hut had been built. Jamal didn't want the kitchen to burn down.

'What are you doing? Get out of my kitchen!' The voice boomed out of the darkness. The voice was like the cook's voice, only different. It was slower and more mixed up. Jamal wasn't sure but he thought it was probably the cook.

'It's me,' Jamal called. 'Are you OK? You sound sick. Shall I fetch someone?'

'Ah, it is my friend Jamal.'

The cook sounded much less frightening now. His words were still slurred but he sounded much happier.

'You should be in your bed, young man, not here creeping round the kitchen.'

There was a glugging sound before the cook started talking again.

'You are hungry, are you? Yes, you're a growing boy, but you shouldn't be in the kitchen at night. I should tell the soldiers and they will beat you and send you to bed.'

Jamal was worried; he hadn't been beaten since he left home and he wanted it to stay that way.

'No, sir, I just wanted …'

'You just wanted something to eat, I bet. Well, my friend, we shall help each other. I will give you something to eat and you will not tell anyone what you saw. Shall we help each other, eh?'

Jamal wasn't sure what he was supposed to have seen, or not seen, but he thought that the food would be good for his journey so he said yes.

'Here, have some plantain chips, and I have these special biscuits. They give them to the hungry – they're very good, but very expensive, they don't give me many. Do you have chips? No? Yes? Here, have some. And look – I have onions! Take an onion, take three.'

The cook piled food into Jamal's arms. Suddenly the cook's legs seemed to fold up and he sat on the floor again. He started to cry.

'Get out of here. Get out!' he shouted at Jamal, waving a bottle in the air. 'I will lose my job and it will be your fault. Get out, GET OUT!'

Collecting Things

Seeing the cook hadn't helped very much. No answer had been given to any of Jamal's questions. And now Jamal had a cupboard full of raw onions. He didn't want to throw them away but was worried that the cleaners would smell them when they came to sweep the room.

Next morning he wandered into the compound. He was going to try to ask the cook about Anof-anage, but when he got to the kitchen the cook was still unwell. He was sitting down, holding his head and moaning and Afiba was serving breakfast. It was Koko, Jamal's favourite, thick and sweet and served with extra evaporated milk. Afiba gave Jamal double helpings but he was too busy to talk. It was good to have a friend in the kitchen.

'Come back at ten,' Afiba said. 'I'll have finished work and Cook will be asleep, so I will be able to leave the kitchen.'

Jamal promised he would and took his breakfast to one of the tables. He sat on his own; he wanted to think about how to get the things on his list and he didn't want anyone to notice that he had extra in his bowl. Just in case Afiba got into trouble.

'The first thing I need is a good strong bag,' thought Jamal, sucking on his spoon until all the sticky porridge was gone.

'And why would a boy in hospital need that?' It was the woman with the tired voice. She had been talking to one of the soldiers. Jamal thought she must be able to read his mind and was worried – perhaps she was a witch. What else did she know about him?

'You said you needed a good strong bag, Jamal, but you haven't told me why.'

What a relief – she hadn't read his mind, he'd been thinking aloud.

'For the trip to Anof-anage. I will need to take my clothes and my book and all my things there. Then I will need the bag to take everything back to Grandfather's and that's a long walk, so it needs to be a strong bag.'

'OK, OK,' she said. 'I get the picture. You really do need a good strong bag. I'll see what I can do.' She shook her head. 'I have never met such a serious boy,' she said. 'He'll change the world, that one.'

'For better or worse?' asked the soldier.

'I wish I could say.'

They both looked back at Jamal and laughed before turning towards the offices.

That was close, thought Jamal. *But at least the bag's sorted.* What else? Drinks, he'd definitely need drinks, but drinks would be difficult as there was only tea and water in the hospital. A blanket would be easy, and his pyjamas and clothes and more food, definitely more food. Jamal was sitting and thinking like this when the nice soldier came back into the compound.

She handed Jamal a drink.

'Thought you'd like this,' she said. 'And the sergeant said you need a bag for your stuff.'

Jamal nodded. It was funny – he liked the soldier but he hardly ever spoke to her. Yet she had given him a drink for no reason at all. His uncles had told him never to speak to soldiers or the police in case they decided to beat him and put him in jail. Jamal didn't think that this soldier would beat him, but she did want to send him away, and that was more or less the same as jail. He wondered if his uncles had known much about soldiers after all. *I wonder what else they didn't really know?* Jamal thought.

'I've got an old kitbag in the barracks, will that do?' The soldier's voice broke into Jamal's thoughts. He looked up.

'Yes, sir! That would be very good.' He wasn't quite sure what he should call a woman soldier. His uncle had said that you must always call a soldier or a policeman sir, but this soldier wasn't a sir. But he decided that it was probably best to stick to sir anyway. At least until he could find out for sure.

'It's got a few holes in it, but it should be OK — you're not going far.'

Jamal knew he *was* going far, but maybe if he took a sheet as well as the blanket, he could put that in the bag to cover the holes.

'No, sir, the holes won't matter at all.'

The soldier got up and passed her drink to Jamal.

'Here, finish this for me; I'm about to go on duty. I'll bring your bag in the morning, and maybe another couple of bottles of Sprite — you may need them to make new friends.'

At ten o'clock Jamal went to find Afiba.

'Not much in the kitchen,' Afiba said, as he threw a mango at Jamal.

'Is the cook still sick?'

'Not as sick as he'll be once the colonel finds out he swapped a side of beef for whiskey.'

'Wasn't it a good swap?' Jamal asked, taking a bite out of the mango.

'Not for him. He'll lose his job by this evening. The minister is visiting tomorrow and he won't eat groundnut stew.' Afiba started laughing, then suddenly went quiet. 'I don't know why I'm laughing. I'll probably lose my job too, if the new boss brings his own kitchen boy with him.'

'That sounds very bad,' said Jamal, 'and unfair. Will the colonel let the new cook do that?'

'The colonel doesn't care about kitchen boys, why should he? But it doesn't matter, I'll find something else. Anyway, what's your news? I hear they're moving you out soon.'

'Yes, I am being sent to a place called Anof-anage till my grandfather comes to collect me. Do you know where that is?'

'Well there's a few, but they usually send kids to St Joseph's, on the other side of the market.'

'I don't understand. How many towns are called Anof-anage? How do people know which one to visit?' Jamal had often been called country boy, as if people from the country were stupid, but he was beginning to think that people from the city were stupid too. Why call lots of towns by the same name?

Afiba started laughing again.

'An orphanage isn't a town, country boy, it's a place, a building. Somewhere to send kids whose parents have died. You must have orphanages in the country, or do they still leave babies in the bush to die?' Afiba kept laughing. Jamal didn't think it was funny at all. How was he supposed to know that in the city you put children in a special building? Why did they do that? Surely there were aunties or uncles or second wives to look after them. Everyone has some relatives. Even Jamal lived with his family, or near his family anyway, and his parents had died. He was about to ask about babies being left in the bush when he realised that Afiba had started talking again.

'... nuns. You'll be baptised and wearing shoes in no time. And that old book of yours'll go; they'll have you reading proper English from a big black Bible.'

'No, they won't do that. I don't belong there.' Jamal was quite keen on the idea of reading, but had no intention of letting his book go. He wasn't sure what being baptised was but he didn't like wearing shoes so he guessed he wouldn't like being baptised either. He was definitely going to have to leave, not just before they found his grandfather, but before they moved him to the orphanage. He needed to go straight away. He decided to share his plans with Afiba.

'I'm not going.'

Afiba just looked at him, waiting for Jamal to explain himself.

'I can't go, I can't. I have to find … I have to be somewhere else … find something, someone. That's where I was going when they brought me here. I can't stay in the orphanage.'

'OK,' Afiba said, as if he had always expected Jamal to run away, 'but you'll have to go from here. You're stuck once you get to St Joseph's. Those nuns keep everyone locked in and they watch you all the time.'

'Will you help me?'

'Yeah, why not. I'll need to think about moving on and now's a good time to go. We can take stuff from the kitchen and the cook will get blamed – he's getting the sack anyway, even if he doesn't know it yet, so it doesn't matter what we take.'

Jamal wasn't sure if this was strictly true, but he didn't say anything. He needed Afiba's help – and anyway, Afiba was much cleverer than he was and was probably right.

Afiba looked up at the clock on the old tower. 'Best be going. Cook will be short-tempered today. I'd better not be late. I'll be busy all day. I will have to do the cooking. I'll have a think tonight and see you tomorrow. Sort out our plans.' Afiba punched Jamal on the arm, in what Jamal thought was probably meant to be a friendly way, then ran off to the kitchen. Jamal wandered back to his room, but was chased out by one of the cleaners.

'Out you, get some fresh air and leave me to do my work,' she said. So Jamal hung around the compound all day, throwing stones at tin cans and trying to catch grasshoppers like his cousins used to do. He wasn't very good at it. He caught them but hated the way their legs scratched and tickled so he opened his hands as soon as he caught them. *Good job I don't need them for lunch*, he thought, *or I'd go hungry again.*

When he finally got into his bed he decided that, even though it had started off well, it had ended up being a very boring day.

Not a Boring Day

The next morning Jamal had a shower before the nurses came round to check if he was OK. He wanted to enjoy the experience for as long as he could, just in case it was the last shower he ever had. Since he had come to the hospital he had showered whenever he got the chance. He would have spent half the day in the showers if he could. Usually someone else was waiting, or the cleaner wanted to scrub the floors, so unless he got up early, his showers had to be very quick. He liked the smell of the soap and the roughness of the towels, but mostly he liked the feel of all that clean water pouring down his back. He thought that maybe this was how it would feel if you lived under a waterfall.

Did the river sprites from the stories feel like this? he wondered. If they did, Jamal was sure that they would not be like the spirits who came to worry him and make him shake. Jamal would never have to worry anyone if he lived under a waterfall. Maybe that was why the spirits had left him alone since he'd been in the hospital. Jamal decided that he would have a shower as often as he could to keep the spirits away.

'Hey, you, have you washed yourself down the drain? Leave some water for me, boy. We all need to get clean.'

Jamal woke up – well, he didn't wake up exactly because he hadn't been asleep. He was quite awake; he'd just been thinking about the wrong things. He turned off the shower and dried himself quickly. A bit too quickly, really; he was still damp when he got dressed and his shorts stuck to his knees as he pulled them up.

'Sorry, sir,' he said, as he dodged out of the shower, leaving a trail of wet footprints on the corridor as he ran to his bed.

The nurse was waiting when he got there.

'Breakfast, then back here. You need a thorough check before you leave us.' She pushed Jamal towards the door. 'A haircut as well, I think, or they'll put you in the girls' room when you get to the orphanage.'

More problems, thought Jamal. How many rooms would there be and why would his hair make a difference? He ran his hand over his damp hair. *Feels*

OK to me, he thought. He didn't think about his hair for long, though, as he could smell breakfast and that was much more important than haircuts or rooms at the orphanage.

'The rooms don't matter cause I won't be there.'

'Where won't you be?' asked the cook. He was back at work, trying to look twice as busy as he really was. 'If you're not here you won't want breakfast, so get out of line and let me serve other people.'

Jamal realised that he'd been thinking aloud again. He didn't used to do that, or maybe he did. He'd been on his own before so no one would have noticed, but now there was always someone about listening to what he was thinking.

'No, sir. I do want my breakfast. I was thinking about the orphanage, sir, and how I hope the food will be as good as yours.'

'Eh? You're talking nonsense. What has that got to do with not being here? Are you leaving today? Good thing, you'll stop distracting my kitchen boy.' He sounded cross but he was smiling. Jamal thought he'd better keep talking just in case the cook got really cross.

'The nurse says I must have a haircut today so I won't go to the girls' room at the orphanage, so I might not be here for lunch.' Not really the truth but sort of nearly truthful. No one could actually say that he'd lied.

'Good job too,' said the cook. 'Better feed you up if you're leaving us.'

He put an extra serving in Jamal's bowl.

'There might even be bean cakes for supper.'

Jamal took the bowl and was about to go back and tell the cook how much better he looked, but he remembered the nurse and ate his breakfast as fast as he could, then ran back to his bed.

'You must be ready to leave us,' said the nurse. 'Every time I see you now you're running somewhere. Now let's go and see the doctor.'

She took Jamal's hand and they walked across the compound to the doctor's office.

The doctor looked in Jamal's eyes, in his ears and down his throat. He measured Jamal and weighed him, listened to his chest and banged his back. Then he turned to the nurse.

'Eating OK? Bowels? Pee?' Jamal didn't quite understand why the doctor asked the nurse instead of him. The words weren't difficult. The doctor did talk with a strange accent – almost everyone in the compound did – but Jamal had got used to that. He hardly ever had to ask people what they meant any more. *The doctor must believe that I'm very stupid,* Jamal thought, *if he thinks I don't know if I've been to the bathroom or not. Living with adults can be so strange.*

'Just the one problem then. You understand that you are a very sick boy?'

Jamal did not understand this at all, but he was quite pleased that the doctor actually spoke to him instead of to the nurse.

'No, sir. I am not sick. I am very well indeed. I am very strong and I have grown taller since I came here.'

The doctor frowned. Instead of answering Jamal he started talking to the nurse again.

'Has no one explained the epilepsy to him, nurse?'

'No, doctor. He is simple, he cannot even read. He has a book that he carries around with him but he cannot understand that it contains words. He would not understand, doctor.'

'Well, let's try, shall we? Jamal, you have been very sick. You *are* very sick. You have something called epilepsy. We give you medicine every day and it stops you from being ill, but you will only stay well if you keep taking the medicine. Do you understand that, Jamal?'

Jamal understood what he said, so he nodded his head. What Jamal didn't know was why he said it. Jamal would have known if he was sick, and he wasn't. He had told the doctor that he was very well and very strong. So Jamal decided that the doctor might be simple. He decided to agree with the doctor so that he wouldn't become upset. He was sure that simple people got upset very easily.

'Up till now, Jamal, the government has paid for your medicine. They've paid for all your care while you've been with us. That is because of the terrorist attacks. Is this clear to you?'

The doctor was talking about the same tribe that the soldier had talked about. Who were these terrorists and where did they live? Jamal did not have a clue what the doctor was talking about but he remembered that the doctor was simple and that he should be nice to him. And so Jamal nodded his head again.

'That is good. See, nurse, he is quite capable of understanding.'

The nurse shook her head, but didn't say anything.

'Now, Jamal, when you leave here the government will not provide your medicine. Do you understand?'

'Yes, sir.'

'You must take your medicine and your grandfather must buy the medicine for you. Do not let him take you to the witchdoctor because a witchdoctor cannot make you well. Only the medicine from a real doctor can make you well and you must take it every day. Can you remember that, Jamal? Every day.'

Jamal said that he could.

'Now, Jamal, I haven't met your grandfather. Will he buy the medicine for you?'

At last an easy question and one he could answer truthfully.

'No, sir. I am quite sure that my grandfather will not buy any medicine. He is a very poor man, sir. He doesn't even grow his own food, sir.'

'Are you sure about that, Jamal?'

'Oh yes, sir. I am quite sure that he is a poor man. But even if he were a rich man he would not buy any medicine for me, sir. He does not like me, sir. He said so. I am not sure he will even come to collect me, even if the soldiers fetch him. He does not like me at all.'

The doctor looked at Jamal as if he'd never heard a boy talk like this before.

'Is this true, nurse? Do we know anything about his family?'

'No, doctor, we know nothing at all. But I hear the boy said something similar to the judge.'

The doctor looked at Jamal again.

'We'll have to sort something out before he goes,' he said. 'The seizures could kill him if they're not controlled. Don't let him leave us until I've discussed his case. In the meantime, make sure he can take his meds without help.'

The doctor went back to the papers on his desk, drawing patterns on them. He saw Jamal looking at him, but he didn't say goodbye. *I was right,* thought Jamal, *he* is *simple – he doesn't even know how to be polite.* Jamal felt very sorry for the doctor.

'Now,' said the nurse. 'What about that haircut? Have you been to the barber before or did your mother cut your hair?'

Jamal was about to tell her that the Imam would shave his head when he visited because his family didn't want to touch him but he didn't get the chance. The nurse took Jamal's hand and led him out of the compound. *I suppose,* he thought, *that nurses are very brave, because they don't mind touching me.* He wondered if they understood about the spirits. Probably not. After all, there had been no spirits since he had been in the hospital.

A Trip to Town

J amal didn't remember arriving at the hospital compound and he hadn't left the compound since then. He was excited to be going into the town and planned on finding out more about the place. Also, he decided to look for signs of the ghosts when he was outside the compound; it might help him work out where to go when he left the hospital. He had never wandered far from his home before the ghosts came and the only other person he had spoken to on his walk was his grandfather. He had seen other people, lots of other people, but Jamal decided that he wasn't going to count dead people. Counting them might make them more real and he preferred to think of the ghosts and the people and his auntie falling in the fire as a sort of enormous dream. He didn't remember actually dreaming since he arrived at the hospital, but that was probably a good thing. There were things that Jamal didn't want to dream about ever again.

'Do not let go of my hand,' the nurse said to him.

She didn't need to say anything. Jamal had never seen so many people, even dead people, and the people here were very much alive. Alive and shouting. Jamal thought the whole town was shouting, each person a little louder than the next. The hospital had been so quiet and the town was so loud. He wanted to cover his ears with his hands, but that would have meant letting go of the nurse's hand. He was sure he would get completely lost if he did.

There was something else that Jamal hadn't expected: the smell. The smell was delicious and awful. He could smell every kind of food he had ever eaten, or could ever wish to eat. The problem was that he could also smell every kind of terrible smell that was ever invented. He could smell the sweat of a thousand old men standing in the sun, mixed with the smell of sick goats and fat sheep. All of this was combined with the smell of waste: rubbish, animal dung and things that Jamal didn't want to think about. How could a place smell so terrible and so good at the same time?

Just as Jamal was beginning to enjoy the noise and the colours and the confusion, the nurse halted at a stall, so Jamal stopped looking around and concentrated on what she was saying.

'For him. Your best price now, no games.'

Jamal wondered why they had paused at such a boring stall.

'The size I've got,' said the stallholder, 'but he's not worn shoes before, has he? He'll complain – you know that, don't you? Don't blame my shoes and come here asking for your money back. His feet aren't used to shoes.'

The nurse and the old man argued for a while then the nurse gave the man some money and the man gave the nurse some shoes. *Funny,* thought Jamal, *they don't look like the sort of shoes she wears.*

'Where next?' he asked.

But they walked only a few steps and stopped at an even more boring stall.

'Socks, vests, underpants, all for him,' said the nurse.

A very fat lady was in charge of this stall. She looked about the same age as the nurse and they chatted and laughed as if they were sisters. If they were sisters they weren't close sisters, thought Jamal. Maybe the same father or maybe the same milk mother, but not close sisters, not like his cousins Teya and Teema. He felt a bit sad thinking about his cousins. They used to laugh just like these two women. He missed them.

'Got his shoes yet?' asked the woman from the underwear stall. 'Then let him put them on. You never know what's on the floor round here.'

The nurse pushed Jamal behind the stall, still chatting as she did so. Then, while Jamal sat on a little stool, she wiped his feet with an old cloth and put the socks and shoes on him. Jamal was not very pleased. No one had asked him if he wanted shoes and he was sure that he didn't. How would he know where he was going if he couldn't feel the road? He did like how the shoes looked, he just didn't like how they felt.

'Now, cousin, doesn't he look smart?'

That explained everything, thought Jamal: not sisters but cousins. Jamal knew that cousins didn't have to look alike – they didn't even have to be related really, just part of one of those families that twisted in and out of each other. A bit like his family.

'Now let's sort out that hair, shall we?' said the nurse. 'Then maybe we can get some tea and a little something sweet.'

They went to a barber's shop where a man with electric clippers took all the hair from Jamal's head. It was a very strange feeling. When he'd finished, Jamal ran his hand over his head – it was completely smooth. He liked his haircut much more than his shoes.

They went to another stall for tea and sweet cakes. Jamal rubbed his head when they sat down and again when they stood up to leave. He was very happy with the feel of his soft, smooth skull. He was very happy about almost everything, except the shoes, and the fact that he would soon be sent to the orphanage.

When they got back to the hospital, the cook said that he looked good with his new haircut.

The cleaner told him how smart he looked in his new shoes, and the soldier had left a kitbag on his bed. She had even left six bottles of Sprite and two bottles of Coke inside. Jamal had never had a bottle of Coke so he thought he would try it, just to see what it was like. He decided it was his favourite drink in the whole world. He sat on the bed next to the soldier's bag and drank the whole bottle. Then he burped. It was so loud that the nurse ran into the room to see what was wrong.

Jamal was sure that this had been the best day of his life. It would have been perfect if it wasn't one day closer to when he had to leave.

Every Time It's Easier

That night, two important things happened. The first was when the cleaner left a laundry trolley by Jamal's bed when he was called away. Jamal changed his own sheets, tucking the old one in his locker, then he changed another two beds, so the cleaner wouldn't know which sheet was missing. He told himself that it wasn't really stealing because he took the sheet from his own bed. Deep inside, though, he knew it was. Stealing had got easier and easier, but he still expected to be found out and punished. Maybe the cleaner would tell the soldiers and they would lock him up in jail. Maybe the nurses would send him straight to the orphanage and tell the nuns to keep him locked up. Or worse, maybe the spirits were watching, even though they had left him alone since he'd been in the hospital. And if they were watching they would definitely punish him, they always did.

The second important thing was that the nurse taught him about his medicine. Jamal hadn't realised how much medicine he had been taking. For the little drinks that he was given every evening turned out to be medicine. Jamal had thought that he hadn't been taking any medicine because the nurses had never told him to take any pills. *These nurses are very sneaky,* he said to himself. He learnt that the medicine made him sleepy and he had to be sure he was somewhere safe before he drank it. Jamal wondered what counted as safe. Did he have to be in bed, or could he just be sitting under a tree? The nurse said, 'Don't be silly, just make sure you're safe, you understand?'

Not next to a fire then, and not near Grandfather either, thought Jamal.

He learnt that he had to take the medicine after breakfast and after lunch and at bedtime and each time he went to sleep.

'What happens if I don't have breakfast?' he asked. 'Or what about if I can't get any lunch?'

'Don't be silly, Jamal. Just take the medicine after your meals like you are told.'

Jamal didn't think he was being silly. He could think of plenty of times when there was not enough food for everyone to have breakfast and quite a few times when there was not enough food for lunch either.

He wondered if the nurse had ever gone without breakfast. Probably not, he thought; she looked as if she had a larder full of food at home.

The next thing she told him was that his medicine must be kept in the fridge.

'What happens if there is no fridge?' he asked.

'Then you must throw that medicine away and buy some more,' the nurse said. 'And you must have a generator – the fridge needs to work all the time, not just when the electricity is on. You understand? Tell your grandfather he must buy a generator.'

Jamal wanted to laugh. He thought of the mountain where his grandfather lived, his smelly cave and the steep climb to get there. There was no electricity on the mountain, and no chance of dragging a generator up there, even if Grandfather could have afforded one. There was a fridge in the kitchen where the cook kept the meat, another in the room where the nurses had their tea and he'd seen a fridge in the coffee shop that they went to in the town. They were the only fridges he had seen. He didn't know if they had generators in the coffee shop, but there was a big generator on the compound. The watchman turned it on whenever the electricity from the town shut down. He was always trying to fix it, pouring oil here or tightening a bolt there, coaxing it until it roared into life and puffed black smoke into the night like the other generators. Grandfather wouldn't be able to do that. He would just throw stones at the generator if it didn't work and throwing stones wouldn't help – it never did. Overall, he thought, taking medicine could be much more complicated than it seemed. He decided that he would never be able to look after the medicine like the nurses did.

'I'll give you the medicine tonight,' said the nurse. 'Tomorrow I'll watch you while you take it yourself.'

Jamal felt worried. If the medicine was very important like the nurse said, why hadn't it been important when he lived at home? And what about the fridge and the safe place and breakfast and lunch?

'What will happen if I don't take the medicine?' he asked.

'You must take your medicine. You must take it exactly how you have been told.'

'Yes, but what if I don't? What happens then?'

The nurse bent down so her face was very close to his. She looked at him very hard then said, 'You must take your medicine, Jamal. You must take it every day and you must keep it in the fridge. You will be very sick if you don't take it. It will not work if it isn't kept cold. You must take it every day, Jamal. Do you understand?'

Jamal nodded. He understood, he just didn't think it would be possible.

Then the nurse patted Jamal's cheek. 'Well done,' she said, and smiled at him.

She showed him how to measure just the right amount of medicine, then she watched him drink it. He had planned on only pretending to drink it, but the nurse was watching him so he took his medicine and went to sleep almost straight away.

He woke up when it was dark. He always did. But instead of going back to sleep Jamal got up and went into the compound. If he was going to leave before he got sent to the orphanage he would have to work out the right time to go. Afiba might change his mind about helping. So he had to make plans on his own, just in case. The best time to leave would definitely be at night. Almost everyone was asleep, except the night watchman and the guards at the main gate. But Jamal thought that the guards might not be that good at staying awake if no one was watching them. He decided to go and check.

He had no problem getting from his bed to the door. The door was closed, but not locked, so he slipped into the compound without making a sound. There were lights in some of the rooms but no noise, so he guessed that the lights had been left burning overnight. It wasn't really dark though, not dark like it was at home. Outside the compound the town was full of lights. It was full of noise too – the people there didn't seem to sleep at night. They must be more like bats or bush-babies, hunting at night for easy prey. Jamal wanted to know how easy it would be to leave the compound; he wasn't ready to think about how he'd get across the town, or where he'd go after that.

As he walked across the compound the dogs lifted their heads and the chains on their necks rattled. But the dogs were used to Jamal so they settled back down to sleep, more interested in their dreams than why a small boy was walking about in the dark. He reached the entrance to the compound. The big metal gate was locked. So was the small gate by the watchman's hut. What was worse, the watchman was awake. Jamal hadn't expected that. He shone his torch towards Jamal.

'Hey, you, what are you doing?'

The light shone right in Jamal's eyes and he stood still; he couldn't see anything but its glare.

'Why are you out of bed, boy? You shouldn't be here.'

Jamal stood quite still. He didn't know what to do. The watchman had always seemed so lazy, sleeping in the shade and chewing betel all day, but now he was wide awake, and there was someone else in his hut. Jamal couldn't see who, but the watchman had spoken to someone when he left the hut, before he shut the door and turned on his torch. Jamal had to think of a reason for wandering round the compound at night, and he had to think quickly.

'It's OK, boy, I'm not going to hurt you. I've seen you around, I know you're not a thief. Go back to bed now. Go back to bed.'

Jamal let his breath out. He hadn't realised he'd been holding his breath but now he wasn't frightened he took great gulps of air. Then he turned around and ran back to his bed. Now he'd been seen he wasn't trying to be quiet and he slammed into the door to the ward. A nurse – one he hadn't seen before – was waiting for him. Jamal thought that the nurse would be cross, but she wasn't.

'Having bad dreams? Guess you're worried about all the changes, eh?'

Jamal nodded his head and shivered a little. It had been damp outside and, suddenly, he wanted to get back into his bed.

'Into bed with you and I'll bring you a drink of tea. That will keep the ghosts and ghouls away.'

Jamal got into bed wondering if the nurse was right and if tea would really send the ghosts back to where they came from. That was something he would have to think about. He snuggled down under the sheet hoping that tea was the answer to his problems.

Another Plan

Jamal woke up very early the next morning, before it was even light. Too early to go down for breakfast, too early even to have a shower. Instead he went for a walk outside to think about what the nurse had said. He wanted to work out if tea really did keep the ghosts away. Jamal sat under his favourite tree and considered. It was true that he had drunk tea more often since he had been in the hospital. It was also true that he couldn't remember seeing any trace of the ghosts since he'd been there. So maybe the tea *was* keeping the ghosts away.

The problem, Jamal thought, was that lots of other things had changed since he'd been at the hospital. There was enough food to have breakfast every day, so maybe it was breakfast that kept the ghosts at bay. Plus he had drunk the medicine that made him sleepy.

Therefore it could have been the medicine which saw them off. Or maybe they simply didn't come when he was asleep.

Jamal sat going over everything that had happened. He remembered that the first time the ghosts had appeared he had been asleep in his hut. And so it wasn't sleep which stopped them coming.

He stopped thinking then and went outside. It wasn't quite dawn but the early animals had started to wake and there were parrots streaming across the sky. Outside, the town was waking up as well. The cars and the horns and the shouts of people in a hurry were all getting louder as the sky was becoming lighter. The watchman unlocked the small gate, then he fetched his mat and left the hut for his morning prayers.

'This is the time to go,' said Jamal. 'Not in the night when people are on the lookout for thieves but early in the morning when everyone's busy.' He said it out loud, but, of course, no one heard him. Everyone was busy getting ready for the rest of the day and no one had time to notice what other people were doing. Jamal went back inside and had a nice long shower before anyone else was up. He got dressed then went out for breakfast.

'You got the weight of the world on your shoulders this morning? Or isn't my cooking up to scratch?'

Jamal smiled at the cook's joke and took an extra couple of bean fritters to go with his bowl of Koko. It was a perfect breakfast.

'No complaints, Uncle,' he said. 'See, I'm taking extra just to prove it.'

Afiba winked at him from behind the cook.

'The *akara* are good,' he whispered. 'I made them myself.'

It was true. Jamal had no complaints about the breakfast, or about any of the meals. In fact, Jamal thought that the cook was probably the best cook in the world, or maybe the second best if Afiba had made the bean cakes. That was part of the reason he had felt so miserable when he came out for breakfast: Jamal knew how much he'd miss all this food when he left.

When he went back inside the nurse was waiting for him. She watched as Jamal took the correct bottle of medicine out of the little fridge, poured the right amount of the pale green liquid into the tiny cup and drank it down in just the right way. Then, before he went to rest on his bed he hugged the nurse.

'Are you feeling OK, Jamal? You've not felt the need to hand out hugs before.'

The nurse sounded surprised.

'Just wanted to say, well, I'll sort of miss you.'

The nurse shook her head.

'Well I never. I didn't expect that. But you're not off yet, young man. Not till I'm quite sure you've got the hang of your meds, and one dose won't do that.'

The nurse pulled down the mosquito net over Jamal's bed then went off to see to her other patients, humming quietly, like she always did.

Jamal lay on his bed, wishing that he could stay in the hospital. He knew he couldn't – even if he didn't leave they would send him to the orphanage in a day or two. Worse than that, they might find his grandfather, and if the soldiers scared him enough, he might actually take Jamal back to the mountain. Jamal tried to imagine what would happen if he had to leave with his grandfather; he was just thinking how awful it would be when, thankfully, he fell asleep.

He didn't get up straight away. He lay in bed, looking at the insects hitting the mosquito net above his head, and thinking. He thought of lots of things that might happen, but none of them ended with Jamal being happy. He knew that if he was going to leave it had to be tomorrow morning, he just wished he didn't have to go. But that was the only way he was going to find the ghosts and stop anything else going wrong. He didn't really believe that last bit. It seemed to Jamal that everything always went wrong, at least for him.

When he finally got up he packed his bag, trying to think of everything he might need for his trip. When other people were about he wandered into the compound and sat under the tree.

Questions, Questions

When he saw the soldier, he asked her about the terrorists.

'Don't you worry about them. They're all up in the north. You're safe now, Jamal.'

Jamal had wanted to know more about the terrorists. Did the ghosts live near the terrorists? Did the terrorists know how to control them? Maybe the terrorists were trying to catch the ghosts as well. Jamal wondered if he should be trying to find the terrorists instead of the ghosts. He knew he had to get some answers and he only had the rest of the day to get them.

After lunch he went to find Afiba.

'Where do people stay when they come to this town?'

'Well, that depends on who they are.' He passed Jamal a plate of fried plantain. 'If you are rich you might stay at the George or the Eko or maybe at the Palace. Would you like me to book you a suite, sir?' Jamal knew that Afiba was laughing at him but he didn't mind. Afiba was always laughing at him, or he was laughing at Afiba. *I wonder if that's what happens when you're friends,* he thought. He wasn't sure – he couldn't remember having had any friends – but Afiba was how he imagined a friend would be.

'No, I'll stay here tonight, maybe even tomorrow, but I need to know where to stay if I don't like the orphanage.'

Afiba laughed and slapped Jamal's back so hard that some of the plantain flew out of his mouth.

'How about poor people, like you or the cook?' Jamal managed to say. 'Where do they stay?'

Afiba stopped laughing. The cook was walking behind him and had overheard what he said.

'I am not a poor person. I have a good job and so does my wife. Mind what you say.'

'Sorry, sir, so sorry, I didn't mean, I only …'

'It's OK, I know you didn't mean any harm. But you must be careful. People aren't poor just because they don't stay at the George. Maybe they just don't get the same bribes as the people who stay there, eh?'

The cook looked at Jamal again and made a sort of tut-tut-tut sound through his teeth.

'I don't know why you're asking. You'll be in a nice warm bed at the orphanage, but the people who come in from the villages, they stay on the lagoon, in Makoko. But that's not a place you want to go. You stay at St Mary's or St Joseph's with the other boys. And don't let your grandfather go to Makoko either. Hear what I say: it's not a place for people like you.'

Jamal was about to ask why he shouldn't go to Makoko but the cook was getting fed up with questions and went back to his kitchen.

Jamal was sitting under the tree to finish the plantain when the woman with the tired voice reached over his shoulder and took one of the crispy treats.

'I hear you're getting ready to leave us,' she said. 'Any questions before you're off?'

Jamal had lots of questions, but he started with what was confusing him most.

'What's Suntmarys? Cook says I'm going there, or Sunjosufs, but I thought I was going to the orphanage.'

'St Mary's is one of the orphanages, so is St Joseph's. There are loads of them in the city, but St Mary's and St Joseph's are the two closest – you'll go to one of those, whichever has a place. We'll let you know on Friday. St Mary's is west of here, St Joseph's is further south. But they're pretty much the same. Why do you want to know?'

'Just something Cook said.'

'Pleased to sort that out for you. Anything else you need to know? For some of your plantain I might be persuaded to share my knowledge.'

'Well, where is Makoko and why mustn't I go there? And where will I get more medicine when mine runs out and what happens if they can't find my grandfather and where do the terrorists live and how do they know about the ghosts and…?'

'Stop, stop, stop! One question at a time. Right then.' She started counting off on her fingers.

'One: Makoko is south of here, next to the lagoon and on the lagoon and maybe under the lagoon as well, for all I know.

'Two: There are lots of reasons you shouldn't go there but let's go with the most obvious – it's very big and you'd get lost.

'Three: You will have to visit a doctor to get more medicine, but you won't have to worry about that till you leave the orphanage; they will arrange all that for you until your grandfather gets here.

'Four: If they can't find your grandfather then you'll stay at the orphanage and go to school there.

'What was the other one?'

'The terrorists,' said Jamal, 'and the ghosts. I want to know about ghosts and terrorists.'

'That's more difficult. I'm afraid no one knows where the terrorists live – if only we did. And I don't know about ghosts. Not really my field. I've turned a few people into ghosts though, but that's *my* business. Now stop worrying, everything's going to be fine.'

She walked away, popping another plantain chip in her mouth as she went.

'What on earth is going through that boy's head?' she said, to no one in particular.

Jamal wondered if she knew more about ghosts than she had told him. After all, she had said she knew how to make them, and if she wasn't talking to ghosts she must have been talking to herself. But Jamal didn't think she would do that.

'What is it with you and ghosts?' Afiba asked. 'The problem with you, boy, is you don't live in the modern world. You don't have a mobile, you don't have a fridge, you don't even have a bicycle, and you still believe in all that old stuff – witches and ghosts and bush spirits. It isn't real, country boy. There are no spooks or trolls or curses.'

'What do you know?' Jamal shouted. 'What do you know about spirits? How they catch you and how you fall down and how you get scratched and bruised and how they bite your tongue and…' Jamal stopped and looked at his friend. 'You don't know anything about spirits; I'm the one they come to – they leave *you* alone.' Jamal got up and turned away from Afiba. He didn't want his friend to know he was going to cry. How could Afiba think like that? Why didn't he understand?

'I'm going,' Jamal said. 'You need to work. You must be too busy to spend time with a stupid country boy like me.'

'Hey, Jamal, come back, I didn't mean it. Maybe you're right, maybe all that magic stuff is true. Come on, Jamal, we've got plans to make.'

But Jamal didn't turn round; he went to his room, letting the screen door slam behind him.

The rains were late, and the afternoon was hot and steamy and Jamal decided to rest on his bed. He didn't intend to go to sleep, though if he was getting up early tomorrow it wouldn't have mattered if he had. But he wanted to be on his own. He had thought Afiba was his friend. He thought Afiba understood, but he didn't. He was just like everyone else, trying to make him feel small. Jamal decided to spend the afternoon planning his next move.

As he pulled down the mosquito net a nurse put her head round the door.

'You tired, Jamal?'

'Yes, Auntie. Can I ask you a question?'

'You can ask, but I might not be able to answer. What do you want to know?'

'Which way is south?'

The nurse pointed towards the big gate that led out of the compound.

'But you sure you want south? I think you want north-east from here. You should ask the watchman — he'll know, for his prayers.'

Jamal just looked at her. Why had she answered a different question to the one he'd asked? People in the city were strange, he thought.

The nurse went off to the tea room with her friends.

'What a strange little boy. I wonder what the nuns will make of him?'

Leaving Home Again

Jamal had decided that he wasn't going to talk to Afiba again, but Afiba came and found him.

'We have to leave tonight,' Afiba whispered. 'I heard them talking – they've found out about the meat, they've sacked the cook. He's gone. I have to make pepper stew for supper and the colonel is taking his visitors to the Palace. Tomorrow there will be a new cook and a new kitchen boy.'

'No, not tonight. We can't leave at night, the watchman will see us. We have to go in the morning.'

'Jamal, think about the new cook – he'll be here in the morning.'

'Yes, but not until breakfast time – we will be gone by then. Trust me, Afiba, we cannot leave at night.'

Afiba sat down on Jamal's bed, ducking under the mosquito net.

'You may be right, but we would have to go very early, before dawn.'

Jamal disagreed. 'No, not before dawn – just after, when the watchman goes to pray.'

Afiba stopped looking worried.

'You've really thought about this, haven't you? You know, country boy, you're not so stupid after all.'

'What about supplies?' Jamal asked.

'Leave that to me. I'll take what I can before they come to check the stock in the kitchen – I've already started. Do you have a bag?'

Jamal said that he did and they agreed to meet up after supper to finish their plans. In the meantime, Jamal would collect something from the kitchen every time he passed.

Afiba got up, ready to return to his chores. When he reached the screen door he stopped.

'Sorry,' he said, 'about this morning. I didn't mean anything. It's just things are different here. More modern, more scientific, you know? Doesn't mean you're wrong; it's just different.'

'Yeah,' said Jamal, 'I know I can't blame you, not if you've never seen a ghost.'

The rest of the day was a sort of dream. Mealtimes and rest times and packing and talking all seemed mixed up together. That night was more like a nightmare. Jamal didn't want to go to sleep, just in case he overslept. But he didn't want to stay awake either. He knew that he needed to be wide awake when he left the hospital. So he spent half the night trying to stay awake and the other half trying to sleep, but dreaming that he should be awake. When he heard the morning noises coming through the windows he was already dressed and hiding in the shadows where he could see the watchman's hut. At first, he sat on his kitbag, but his eyes began to close so he stood up with his bag propped against the wall. After a while he too leant against the wall. He was thinking about how to keep from falling asleep when Afiba appeared out of the shadows.

'Hey, Jamal!'

'Shh, the watchman's still about. You ready?'

'Ah, well, the thing is ... change of plans.'

'But you said we were leaving together. You know where we're going.'

'Hey, chill. It's all arranged. I'm staying so I don't get blamed for the missing food. And my uncle has paid a dash to the new cook, so I get to keep my job.'

'But what will I do?'

'Like I said, it's all settled. You take out the stuff – the food and things – and my uncle will meet you outside. He'll take you across the city. It's much safer.'

Jamal wasn't sure. It sounded safer for Afiba, but not very safe for him. Who would believe him if he got caught? And could he trust Afiba's uncle? Jamal's uncles had told him to trust only the family. But they didn't tell him what to do when there wasn't any family around. What could he do? There was no one else to trust, and he had to leave the compound before they sent him to the orphanage and locked him up.

'OK, OK. What does your uncle look like?'

'No worries, I'll come out with you, help you carry the crate to my uncle's car, then I'll go back to the kitchen. Easy, and everyone wins.' Afiba grinned. For Afiba everything was always easy.

'Come on, Jamal, help me get the crate from the kitchen.'

The two boys wrestled with the blue plastic box; they could just about lift it between them.

'What's in this, Afiba? It feels like you've got half the kitchen in here.'

'Oh, you know, things that won't be missed. A little here, a little there … just things for the family.'

Jamal doubted that the things in the crate wouldn't be missed, but he didn't say anything. It's difficult to say much when you're trying to carry a heavy box without making a sound. When they put the crate down, Afiba took off his backpack.

'Here, stuff for you, a sort of payment for helping me out.' Just then they heard the keys turn in the metal gate. Jamal moved forward and saw the watchman heading towards the prayer room. He lifted his bag onto his shoulders, surprised by how much heavier it was with Afiba's backpack inside. The boys waited a few minutes, just to be sure the watchman wouldn't come back, then they looked round to check that no one else was about. They struggled through the gate with Jamal's bag and the heavy blue crate, then stood panting in the shadows.

A car flashed its lights at the end of the road.

'There!' said Afiba. 'You see, Jamal? I told you he'd be here.'

Afiba picked up his side of the crate. 'Come on, we need to be quick.'

Heading South

Afiba's uncle didn't get out of his car; he just sat there waiting while the boys struggled down the road to where he was parked.

'Hurry, hurry. I don't want to be seen here.' He spat betel out of the window while the boys hauled the crate onto the back seat.

'You, Afiba's friend, you sit in the front so you can get out quickly.'

Jamal did as he was told, pulling his bag in with him.

'Good luck! I hope you find the people you're after,' Afiba said before slamming the door, just as his uncle started to pull away.

It was still early – there was just a hint of yellow behind the clouds – but the roads were crowded. Afiba's uncle cursed the other drivers in ways that Jamal had never heard, but it didn't help: the traffic was packed all around them almost straightaway. Yellow buses and three-wheeled taxis pushed into gaps that were barely big enough for motorbikes. Bikes and scooters wove through spaces that were too small for people to squeeze through and everywhere there were people. Jamal had thought that it was busy when the nurse had taken him to the market, but that was nothing.

'Where do all these people live, Uncle?' Jamal asked.

'So Afiba wasn't joking. He said you were stupid. They live here, of course, in the city. In the old city if they're lucky, down by the lagoon if they're not. And him ...' Afiba's uncle pointed to a huge black car with a policeman at the wheel. 'He lives the other side of the bridge. Not that you'll ever go there so you don't need to worry about people like that. You just need to get out of their way.' He turned the car to the left, where a space opened up between a man with a red umbrella and a bicycle loaded with oil cans. The black car sped past, then all the other cars did the same.

'So, do you want to get out here? There's plenty of people, easy to hide yourself.'

'Not really, sir,' Jamal said. 'I need to head south. We are going towards the sun – isn't that east?'

'More country lore, eh? Well, you can't trust your country knowledge here. But yes, boy, we're going east – that's where I need to be. You get out here, like

I said. It's a good place to hide yourself. If you want to go south, follow the railway line. Even a country boy can do that. Now, out! I want to get home.' He leant across Jamal and opened the car door, almost pushing him onto the street. 'Don't forget, boy, if you're caught don't mention my nephew. If you do, I'll find you.'

He then reversed his car, causing a dozen other drivers to lean on their horns but Afiba's uncle didn't look back.

Jamal stood by the road, holding on to his bag as people bumped and pushed him from every side. This wasn't what he had planned. He wanted to get to Makoko. So many people had told him that he shouldn't go there, that it was a bad place. Jamal thought that it sounded just like the sort of place where the ghosts would be. So he had to go south, to Makoko. Afiba's uncle had said that country rules didn't apply in the city, but that couldn't be true. Not when it came to the sun. The sun was the same wherever you went. Even on the godless mountain, where his grandfather lived, the sun was the same. So Jamal turned his back to the sun then held out his left hand. It pointed across the road to where a market was being set up. That way was south, or it would have been at dawn, so he started walking – not straight across the road, but almost. He couldn't have walked straight across the road even if he'd wanted to; he had to dodge between the cars and taxis, and weave between the other pedestrians. When he was at home it was easy to walk in a straight line. There was nothing in the way, except perhaps a tree or two. Jamal didn't get lost walking round trees but it was much harder to walk in a straight line in the town. Jamal thought that something or someone was in the way every few steps.

He had to turn right when he got to the market and then left when a policeman stopped him so that three black cars could drive by, then he turned right again when he came to a fence covered in spikes. And then he got caught in a crowd and there were so many people that he had to go with them – and then he was lost!

Being lost was bad; being lost and hungry was worse. Jamal was beginning to wish that he'd waited until after breakfast before he ran away from the compound. He hoisted his bag onto his head. It wobbled – he was really bad at carrying things this way – but the bag was too heavy to carry in his arms. *I need to lose some of this weight,* he thought. Then he remembered: the bag was full of food. He decided to find somewhere to stop before trying to find the railway. He was, in fact, very near the railway – the market had been set up next to the tracks – but as Jamal had forgotten to ask what a railway looked like he didn't realise how close he was to his route south.

Jamal didn't want to stop where he was – there were too many people and he was sure that someone would tread on him if he sat down. He walked to where there were fewer people but it turned out that there were fewer people because he'd walked in a circle. He was back at the road where there were hundreds of cars. He decided that there was nowhere quiet to sit, only the seats by the tea stalls, and when he couldn't buy any tea the stallholders chased him away. He would just have to eat while he walked.

He opened his bag, and then he opened the backpack that Afiba had given him before he left. At the top, wrapped in newspaper, were six *moin-moin*, each one soft and round and nestled in its own paper case. Six cakes were too many to eat at once, even for Jamal, who liked cake very much. So he took out two and tucked them in his pockets. Then, just before he tied up the bag again he took out another; after all, it was important to eat a good breakfast. It didn't make the bag much lighter, but as he balanced the bag on his head, he was sure that he would be able to manage the weight better once he had eaten the cakes.

The cakes were good, and when he'd eaten them he remembered that the nurse had said he must take the medicine after his breakfast. He thought about it, but as he looked around he realised that the market wasn't a safe place to fall asleep. *It can't matter if I miss one dose*, he thought. After all, he hadn't taken medicine when he lived at home and he hadn't been sick there. He decided to wait until lunchtime to take his medicine.

He wandered through the market, eventually reaching the edge of the stalls where small stones were piled up to make a long mound. There were concrete blocks arranged on top and long metal bars on the concrete. Lines of people were walking between the metal rods, all going in the same direction, like migrating animals. Jamal stopped still, looking at the people. As he did, an old woman carrying a basket of vegetables bumped into him.

'You going up to the railway or not?'

'Yes, but …'

'Don't worry, it's safe. It's another government mess-up. They built the line, then ran out of money, so they couldn't buy the trains. No trains, no risk. Not like the old railway. You can follow this line all day and never see a train.' She started laughing, a deep chuckle, like the way the nurse laughed when she was talking to her cousin. She pushed Jamal up the slope in front of her, and he joined the people walking down the track.

So, Jamal thought, *I've found the railway, but am I going south? If the railway goes south it must go north as well.* He looked up to find the sun, but the clouds had rolled in – the rains would come tomorrow, or the next day. He tried to turn round but there were too many people heading the same way; he had to walk with them and hope they were all going south.

Jamal walked for about half an hour before he needed to stop. *I've grown soft in that hospital,* he thought. *I used to walk all morning when I lived at home.* But he was thirsty, so he stepped off the concrete path and sat on the stones to drink the soda that the soldier had given him.

The railway went over a river – wider than the river near Jamal's home, wider than three or even four rivers put together. There were boys walking along the wall that ran by the edge of the railway but Jamal stayed right in the centre of the bridge. He felt sick when he thought of falling so far into the water. He was sure the boys would die if they fell, but they didn't seem worried at all. It was as if different things mattered in the city; no one was afraid of cars or fires or falling into the river. *If I ever find the ghosts,* Jamal thought, *they will be very fat, because so many people must die in the city every day.*

Leaving the Railway

There were places where markets were set up next to the railway, and others where the railway was closed in by steep walls, but all the time the track was full of people walking and chatting and looking busy. When Jamal had first got to the railway everyone was walking the same way but by the time the sun was overhead people were coming and going all the time, heading in different directions, sometimes not even keeping to the track itself but crossing over and heading to the buildings on the other side.

Jamal wanted to find somewhere to have lunch, somewhere with a little shade and fewer people than on the railway, so when he saw the next market he decided to try his luck in the city. He dodged between the stalls, the smell of fried peppers and hot soup making his stomach grumble. He realised now that he had become used to living at the hospital where Afiba was always around to give him something sweet from the kitchen.

As he worked his way through the market he saw a blue building rising high above the crowds of people. He didn't know where else to go so he headed for that. It turned out to be a very good plan. When he reached the blue building he saw it was standing next to a field with grass and trees and flowers. He hurried towards it. He was worried about being lost now that he'd left the railway, but he knew he'd feel better if he was sitting under the trees. Trees were good for making you feel calm and this field must have been planted so that all these people could stop rushing and get calm again.

He put his bag next to a tree with flat leaves and red bark that reminded him of the laterite roads in his village. It wasn't like the trees at home, which were short and covered in spines. It was, Jamal thought, the sort of tree that belonged in the city. He sat on the bag and leant against the trunk. Things were not so bad after all. He pulled out an onion and bit into it, wondering why the cook always fried onions when they tasted so much better raw. When he'd finished, he thought about the hospital and wished he could have stayed there. Then he remembered the nurse who had taught him to take his medicine. He fished around in his bag until he found the bottle. Then he put the medicine on the ground while he looked for the measure.

Just then a boy sped past him on a sort of rolling board. He leant over and took the medicine without even stopping.

'Hey!' said Jamal. 'Bring it back! I need it.'

But the boy didn't stop; he just laughed as he drank the medicine straight from the bottle. Before he reached the next tree he threw the empty bottle into a patch of flowers before waving at Jamal in a very unfriendly way.

Jamal left his bag and walked over to the flowers. The bottle wasn't empty, but it nearly was. He carefully wiped the drips then licked his fingers. *It's not a whole dose,* he guessed, but he understood he'd have to take smaller amounts now, as there was so little left. He found the lid and put it back on the bottle so he could save what was there. *What now?* he thought. *Should I go back to the hospital or try to find my way home?* But Jamal was too lost to know which way to go. He had no choice – he had to keep looking for the ghosts.

Jamal put the bottle back into his bag and slouched over to the shade of another tree. *That boy must have been sick too,* he thought, *but still, it was a lot of medicine to drink.* He was worried about the boy and wondered if he ought to tell him about getting tired, but the boy had already left the field. Anyway, after drinking so much medicine Jamal guessed that he'd already be feeling tired. Instead, Jamal decided to rest under the tree and try to work out where he was. He knew that if he waited until evening then he would know which direction was west, but he didn't think that was a good idea. In fact, he thought it was a very bad idea.

First, he would have wasted a whole day.

Second, there were so many buildings that he might not see the sun set.

And third, he didn't know if he still ought to be heading south.

He needed a better plan. He looked around, hunting for anything that might give him a clue. The field he was in was very strange. There were no crops, just trees and flowers. Jamal thought this was a waste of space. If someone planted the field they could save money at the market. The field was big enough for a good harvest; there would even be spare food to sell, if it was a good year. There weren't any animals grazing either, although the animals might have all wandered off. There was no stockade around the field and therefore plenty of places for goats to get lost in. He wasn't sorry that it was just a grassy space – it made a nice place to sit – but he didn't understand why no one had dug up even a little part to plant food.

There were a lot of stone carvings as well. Carvings of people that were bigger than real people. The workers who made them must have been very skilled, which was another odd thing. The carvings that Jamal had seen before were small and badly done, but these were beautiful. The statues of women looked like goddesses and the men like warriors.

Jamal would have liked to spend longer looking at the carvings and working out how they were made but he saw a clue over the left shoulder of one of the giants. He saw ghosts. The thick yellowy-brown smoke that he'd seen snaking out from the red canister at home was rising high above all the buildings. Jamal knew that the smoke wasn't actually a ghost but the ghosts seemed to travel in the smoke. And as there was an awful lot of smoke behind the buildings so there would be an awful lot of ghosts. This smoke didn't hug the ground like the smoke at home. It rose straight up before gradually drifting away. What Jamal didn't know was how long the ghosts would be there. He picked up his bag, ready to follow them, but the bag felt very heavy.

Maybe if I had another drink, and maybe a small snack, the bag would be lighter, he thought. *After all*, he reasoned, *I can watch the ghosts while I'm eating and leave the field quickly if they look like they're going.*

Jamal was pleased with that idea, so he settled on the ground with his back to the giant carvings and ate the rest of the *moin-moin* and another onion and watched the ghosts rising behind the buildings.

Following the Ghosts

Jamal finished his drink and put the bottle back in his bag. He wasn't sure where to leave it and he might need it later. Maybe he could trap one of the ghosts in it. He finished his onion and then a whole bag of plantain chips and then remembered his medicine. There wasn't much left, so he took a sip. He shook the bottle – just one more dose left. Jamal wished he could remember what the nurse had said about getting more, but no matter how hard he tried the words seemed to hide from him. It was like that sometimes, after he'd taken the medicine. He knew he'd have to wait before he could remember things properly again so he put the bottle back in his bag and headed off towards the ghosts.

The ghosts were further away than he'd expected. He walked straight towards them – or at least, nearly straight towards them, because in a city like this there was always a building in the way. He kept walking all afternoon even though he was desperate to go to sleep. By the time the sun went down he didn't seem any closer to the spiral of yellow ghost smoke. He needed somewhere to rest, but he didn't understand the town. He didn't know which places were safe to sleep in and which places were not. He could still see where he was going – the town was full of light. It was full of people too. He wondered if the people who lived here didn't have homes. Maybe they just stayed awake all night, and he saw he would have to do the same. But he was so tired and he didn't know if he'd manage to keep awake, even if the music and the noise didn't stop. He decided to look for somewhere out of the way so he could rest there. He was used to sleeping on the floor and he had a blanket in his bag so he thought he would be OK if only he could find a quiet spot. Jamal took another bottle of Sprite out of his bag and drank it while he was walking. It didn't help: he still felt tired and his bag still felt heavy. He thought about throwing the bag away but it was full of things he might need.

Jamal kept walking. He tripped over his own feet and bumped into the rubbish that was left on the pavement. He thought he would walk better without his shoes, but when he tried to take them off the buckles seemed to wriggle away from his fingers.

Eventually he saw a corner where he fancied he could sleep. It was the doorway of a closed-down shop, dry and dark and hidden looking. The problem was that other people were already there.

'Clear off, little boy.'

'Go back to your mummy.'

'Find your own place.'

He would have to find somewhere else, so he kept walking, trying to find what he needed. He remembered that the cook had said the biscuits were special energy biscuits. Jamal thought that maybe if he ate them he would have enough energy to keep walking. He ate one packet and put the other in his pocket. He wondered if the cook had given him the wrong biscuits because he didn't have any more energy. He knew he had to find somewhere to sleep soon before he fell down and slept in the middle of the road.

Finally he saw six or seven boys, about his age, sitting round a fire. The fire was in an old oil drum and the boys had pulled boxes and drums and even an old car seat around it.

'Can I sleep here? I can't walk any more.'

'If you want to stay, you gotta pay,' chorused the boys. 'What you got to share?'

Jamal dropped his bag on the ground.

'I need my blanket, and my book,' Jamal said. 'And I need my medicine, but you can share the rest. I don't care.'

'What sort of *medicine* is that?' The tallest boy was laughing. 'Palm wine sort of medicine, or maybe beer sort of medicine?'

'No,' said Jamal. 'Real medicine. I have to take it 'cause I'm sick.'

Jamal started to take the things he needed out of the bag. He looked at the medicine bottle. Just one drink left. He tipped up the bottle and drank the last of the green liquid. Then he wrapped his blanket around him and lay down on the pavement.

'That boy *is* tired,' the tallest boy said. 'Here!' The boy threw the empty kitbag at Jamal. 'Better sleep on that. While we help you out by eating this stuff.'

Jamal rolled onto the bag and put his book under his head, like a pillow. He had fallen asleep before the boys had finished sharing out their loot.

Jamal was alone when he woke up. Alone except for a scabby-looking dog that was sniffing his face. He got up quickly, shooing the dog away. He knew wild dogs had rabies and he was afraid of being bitten. The boys had all disappeared, and so had the fire and their seats.

The rest of Jamal's food and all his spare clothes had disappeared with them.

'Go away, dog,' said Jamal. 'It's going to be a hungry morning for both of us and I've got some ghosts to find. Go away, and don't follow me. Go away.'

The dog sniffed the ground where Jamal had been lying but lost interest when he couldn't find any food. Jamal rolled up his blanket and put it, with his book, in the kitbag. The bag was nearly empty so Jamal carried it like a parcel under his arm. It was easier to manage now but he wondered what he would do as the food was all gone.

'Maybe I'll reach the ghosts today,' he said, but the dog had gone off to find breakfast and no one else noticed him. He was just another street boy talking to himself.

Jamal looked around until he saw the yellow smoke, then he headed that way. He seemed to be moving away from the main part of town. The buildings were shorter here, not much higher than normal houses and much less shiny. They were more like the storerooms at the hospital, but not as well built. The roofs were made of tin and the walls were patched. The roads were narrower too, and they weren't as smooth as the ones near the hospital or the field. He

143

wondered how far he had walked last night before he found the boys.

He kept heading for the smoke, walking round black greasy puddles and avoiding piles of rotting vegetables until he could smell the yellow smoke and he knew he must be getting close.

He remembered he had an energy biscuit in his pocket but he left it there. The smell in this part of town made his stomach roll and he didn't want to waste the last of his food if he was going to be sick.

He turned left, and left again when his way was blocked by a lorry full of squawking chickens. Right in front of him was a wire fence, higher than a man and topped with wire that was twisted like a thorn bush. Behind the fence was a hut where a fat watchman sat listening to a radio. Behind that – and behind the three brown dogs with sharp-looking teeth – was a high tower. The yellow smoke was pouring out of the tower and climbing towards the clouds. Jamal realised that this wasn't where the ghosts came from – it was just an old, dirty factory.

No Ghosts, Only Witches

J amal looked at the factory. As he got closer
he could see that the dogs weren't loose but
trapped in a sort of cage between two fences,
keeping them away from the men working in the yard
yet still stopping anyone getting through the wire and
into the factory. Jamal decided that the dogs must be
as vicious as wild dogs if they had to be kept locked
away from everyone, even the watchman. Out in the
yard men were moving crates with little tractors and
rolling oil drums. They all wore thick gloves and hard
blue hats and dirty yellow jackets. The smoke from
the factory smelt as if a whole tray of eggs had been
lying in the sun. This was not the smell that the ghosts
had left in the compound at home. The smell didn't
make Jamal's eyes sting or his throat tighten, it just
made him gag.

Jamal sat on the ground next to the fence – not leaning on the fence in case the snarling dogs could bite through the wire, but close enough so he wasn't near the trucks that came and went through the big iron gates.

Jamal was tired and hungry and no nearer finding the ghosts.

'Get out of here. You, over there. Clear off! Clear off or I'll let the dogs out.' The watchman had come out of his hut and was shouting at Jamal.

'I just need to sit here for awhile. I won't get in the way.'

But the watchman didn't care how tired Jamal was.

'I said get out of here. This is no place for street boys and thieves. Get out.'

Jamal tried to stand up, but his legs seemed to ignore him.

'Please, sir, let me sit here just for a minute. I won't be long and then I'll go and find the ghosts.'

Jamal slumped forward, resting his head on his knees and pulling his bag close. He hadn't had breakfast, or even anything to drink, and he just couldn't walk any more. So he decided that he would stay where he was even if the dogs were let out. He had failed. He had lost his medicine, he had lost his clothes, he didn't know where he was and he still hadn't found the ghosts. Jamal couldn't imagine the day getting any worse. It didn't.

It got better – just a bit. As his hand rubbed against his bag he heard a very quiet rustling sound. He fished into the pocket and found the single squashed energy biscuit, still wrapped in its shiny paper. Had the street boys missed it? Or had they left it for him? He didn't know. He didn't really care. He opened the packet and took a big bite. It was very dry – quite hard to swallow without a drink. But Jamal didn't have a drink, and he didn't think the watchman was likely to give him any water. So he chewed the biscuit and tried to swallow the sweet, peanutty crumbs.

He had eaten half the biscuit when he felt a sharp pain on the back of his head.

'Get out of here, I said.'

The watchman was still angry. He hadn't let the dogs out but he was standing at the gate, holding a bucket and shouting at Jamal again.

Before he'd finished his biscuit something hit his back. Another stone, and then another. Jamal felt blood trickle down the back of his neck. He swallowed the rest of the biscuit quickly, just in case the watchman threw anything else at him.

'Hey. I'm going. It's just, I don't know where to go now.'

'Go back to where you came from. I told you – no thieves here.'

Jamal couldn't understand why the watchman was so angry. But struggled up as a stone hit him. Another stone hit his head and he started to blink as blood ran into his eye.

'I said I was going. Leave me alone.'

The stones stopped when a lorry arrived at the gate and the watchman went over to speak to the driver.

'Can't get rid of those kids; they keep trying to sneak onto the site. Jump on the back of trucks if they get a chance. Takes me all my time to keep them away.'

The watchman and the driver both looked at Jamal as he walked off.

'They need sweeping off the streets,' said the watchman. 'Dumping in the lagoon with the other rubbish.'

Jamal didn't hear what the driver said because he wanted to get away from the watchman and the bucket of stones. He was in a hurry and didn't look where he was going. He bumped into a boy in torn shorts and a dirty football shirt and they both ended up on the ground. The boy looked ready to start a fight, but when he saw Jamal's face he smiled.

'It's the boy with the food. You got any more? Your clothes were good. I didn't get any though. Too small for me, but they fitted the others.'

Jamal still hadn't said anything. He could smell nutmeg and his head was spinning. He knew that the smell was important but he couldn't remember why. The boy was still saying something but he was unable to work out what. The words didn't seem to make sense any more. They twisted round and got mixed up together, like milk and water poured on the floor.

When Jamal woke up, the boys were all standing round him. They weren't looking at Jamal but at a crowd of adults who were shouting.

'Witch, witch, witch.'

Jamal could hear the words but he didn't understand why they were calling for a witch.

'Get rid of him.'

Jamal wondered who they wanted to get rid of. Then he heard the watchman's voice.

'I'll get the dogs; they'll chase him off.'

'We don't need his curses.'

'Get rid of him.'

Jamal tried to get up to have a better look. He wanted to know what was going on.

'Get down!'

Stones and sticks and empty bottles were thrown at the boys. Some hit Jamal, others hit the boys protecting him. But the boys didn't move. They stood there, like a wall between Jamal and the adults.

'Witch, witch, witch.'

Jamal had never heard so many adults sounding so angry at the same time. He was about to ask what was happening when he heard a wailing noise.

'Police!' someone shouted

Everyone started running. A hand reached down and pulled Jamal to his feet. He was pulled and pushed and hustled away from the factory, down a side road. All the boys hid behind a pile of rotting fruit.

Jamal glanced over his shoulder and couldn't believe how empty the street was. The watchman was back in his hut and the other adults had all gone.

'You must have really hit your head hard,' the boy in the football shirt said.

'I've never seen anyone go down like that. All that shaking. Freaked me out.'

'Freaked everyone out,' another boy said. 'You better get out of here. They'll be back when the police have gone, especially the watchman. Got a thing about witches he has. Thinks a witch cursed his wife.'

The boys laughed.

'She just left him for someone who smells better. But he prefers to blame a witch – not the fact he doesn't wash.'

Jamal was worried. He was beginning to feel better but he was also beginning to realise that everyone thought he was the witch.

'I don't know where to go,' said Jamal. 'I was looking for ghosts but only found this factory.'

The boys looked at one another and pulled faces. The sort of faces you pull when someone is talking nonsense.

'You still need to go. You could try the dump. Out by Makoko. If ghosts are going to be anywhere that's the place they'd be.'

The boys nodded, keen to get Jamal to leave before they were all branded as witches.

'You'll be OK there. Follow this road and don't turn off. Even if it looks like other roads are better. Just stay on this road and you'll get to the dump.'

'Yeah, and follow your nose. Smells like the dead out there. Bound to be crawling with ghosts.'

There was a general murmur of agreement from the boys. There was quite a lot of giggling too. They were city boys; they didn't believe in ghosts or witches. Well, maybe they believed in witches a bit, but they weren't going to admit that to each other. Or to anyone else – especially not to a country boy who was clearly fresh off the bus.

Jamal thanked them, and, once they were sure that the adults had gone, the boys slipped out from their hiding place.

'Here,' said one of the boys, passing Jamal a carton of orange juice. 'Not many places to find an unattended drink out there.'

'And you'll pass some mango trees about a mile out. Stop and pick some. Don't eat what you find on the dump.'

The boys ran off before Jamal had time to say thank you, laughing about something. Jamal couldn't hear what they said, but he guessed they were probably laughing at him.

Follow this road, they had said, but which way? Why did people forget to tell you that? Afiba's uncle, for example, and now the street boys too.

Oh well, Jamal thought, *the boys went that way so I'll go this way. If it's wrong I can always come back; I'll only have to follow the smoke.*

He walked along the road and when he was sure that no one was following him he opened the carton of juice. He was pleased that he'd found the biscuit, but he was really happy that he had something to drink.

Learning About Life

Follow the road, the boys had said. That had been easy to start with. But Jamal wasn't convinced that he'd been given the right information. It was a small road, full of rubbish and potholes, and it looked as if it would end in a brick wall. He didn't believe it was really going to take him to the ghosts – more likely it would lead to another kicking. *I should have stayed at home,* he thought. *Nothing good has happened since I left.*

Jamal thought about what had happened: he'd been hungry and thirsty, he'd been kicked and punched and robbed, and he'd been lost. Over and over again he'd been lost. He thought about the hospital. That had been the best place to be. If he could have stayed there, maybe he could have forgotten about the ghosts. Maybe he should have gone to the orphanage. Maybe it wouldn't have been as bad as Afiba said. After all,

Afiba had never actually been to the orphanage; he had just told Jamal tales about it and Jamal knew how tales could grow. First someone heard a noise in the night. Then the noise was a bird landing on the roof, then it was a giant bird, and then a magical bird. Then it wasn't a bird at all, but a spirit or a witch or a demon. The next thing you knew the whole village left their houses and moved to the other side of the hill.

Yes, Jamal thought, *stories always grow.* Maybe he should have gone to the orphanage. But it was too late for maybes. He'd missed his chance and now the best thing he could do was find the ghosts – perhaps things would get back to normal when he did.

By the time Jamal had finished thinking about what he ought to have done he had reached the end of the road. The boys had said follow the road all the way to the dump but there was no dump here, just another road full of traffic and noise and with shops on either side. The shops spilled out onto the road with racks of clothes and piles of buckets and mobile phones in padlocked cases. There were teashops with blue plastic chairs, cages of chickens and piles of vegetables. Everywhere that Jamal had been since he left the hospital people had set up stalls. It was as if the city was one big market. He tried to imagine how many people must live in the city if they needed so many shops and how big the farms must be to produce all the vegetables.

He could go right or left. He looked right and saw a policeman in white gloves walking to where two yellow buses had crashed into each other – he remembered the boys running away from the police cars and decided to go left.

But he couldn't walk straight down the road – it was too crowded. The clothes people were wearing fascinated him. At home, his aunties covered their heads and shoulders with dark scarves and his uncles wore long shirts and loose pants. In the city it was as if people wore whatever they could find, as long as it was bright. There were women with scarves, but the scarves were red or pink or sky blue and purple. But some women didn't wear scarves: they showed their necks and wrapped their hair in bright cloths that matched their dresses. Others didn't cover their hair at all. Even their dresses were different. Some women wore skirts so short that Jamal thought they must belong to small children, while some wore long dresses that swept the ground as they walked. There were men in shorts, men in trousers and plain shirts, and men in T-shirts or no shirts at all. And no one seemed to mind. No one tapped them on the shoulder and said you shouldn't wear this or that. No one was made to wear a hat, or not wear a hat, or shave their head or even grow a beard. Jamal spent more time looking than walking and more time bumping into people than avoiding them.

I haven't got time for this, Jamal thought. But then, what if he found the ghosts and didn't come back this way? He didn't want to miss anything. Looking up, he saw there were people living high above the shops. There were three – sometimes four – storeys above the ground level. Jamal could see people hanging out of the windows, shouting down to the street, telling children to come inside or calling to the street traders below. Jamal had never seen anything like this place. He had never heard anything like it either – the car horns and the shouting and the music in the cafes and the phone shops.

He was looking up, trying to work out how people got their washing onto the lines that stretched across the road when he stumbled and fell into the traffic. Horns blared and people shouted and a hand grabbed Jamal by the arm, pulling him back away from the cars. At the same time three small children pushed against a stall, sending spicy snacks and hot oil all over the pavement. They grabbed what they could in an open basket and ran out into the traffic.

'Thief, thief!' shouted the stallholder. He ran after them, calling all the time and waving his cooking knife over his head.

The person who was holding Jamal's arm let go, and Jamal, still off-balance, fell to the ground – pulling his hand quickly away from the oil.

Other people had taken up the stallholder's cry: 'Thief, thief! Stop thief!'

The children were quick, but the crowd was quicker and the children did not get very far before they were surrounded by angry stallholders. Everyone's attention was on the thieves – even some of the drivers had got out of their buses and cars to join in, making sure that the children could not get away. Well, not everyone's attention was on the thieves: other children had spilled out of the doorways and were scooping up the snacks on the ground. Jamal looked around. He was very hungry but he didn't want to be chased by anyone with a cooking knife.

'Go on,' said a small girl in an embroidered dress. 'It's OK. They were stupid, made a big show. They should have been quicker, a little here and a little there. No one notices small hands.'

'Shouldn't we help them?' Jamal asked.

'No, we just help ourselves. Here, take some. Quick! Before everyone comes back.' She handed Jamal three small snacks. He popped them in his mouth, not bothering to brush off the dirt. When the snacks were gone the children disappeared back into the doorways.

Jamal stood up, taking care not to slip on the oil. There were six more *puff-puff balls* where he had been sitting. He picked them up, putting them in his pockets for later, then he wiped his hands on his shorts. They were his new shorts, the ones which had been bought at the market when his hair had been cut. Only they didn't look new any more. He was beginning to look like the other street children, and he had been in the city for only two days. He wondered how the children ever kept clean. But there was no one to ask. His questions would have to wait. He could see the stallholders returning. Time to go. He squirmed his way along the pavement, this time looking at his feet, not at the buildings.

The Sound of Music

J amal walked until the sun went down. The sun had set but it wasn't dark: lights came on in shops, windows in the houses glowed yellow, and the stalls were strung with coloured lights. And the music! Jamal had never heard so much music. Every shop played music and men were standing on street corners, listening to music, dancing to it. It was as if there were two sets of people in the city – the day people and the night people, like the animals in the bush. Every space was filled twice.

Jamal was definitely a day person, though he wished he wasn't. He wanted to belong to this exciting second city. But his legs ached and his new shoes pinched his toes and, once again, he needed to find somewhere to sleep. He thought about leaving the main road and trying to find somewhere quiet in one of the alleys that snaked between the houses. But there was always someone there before him. Maybe it would have been safe to take an afternoon nap there, but not at night. Jamal almost wished that he was a witch, so he could frighten people away from the best places. But he wasn't, so he just kept walking, hoping that he'd find somewhere.

It was less noisy than it had been: the shops had begun to pull down their shutters and there were fewer stalls by the side of the road. Jamal thought at first that it was because it was so late that even the dancers had gone home, but when he turned around he could see that it looked as if there was a street party behind him. He was walking away from the main part of the city. Now he really did have to find somewhere to sleep. There were fewer lights the further he walked and he was afraid of falling – there were piles of rags and heaps of boxes all over the path ahead. He moved closer to one of the closed shops and tried to clear some space between the rubbish.

'Oi, get your own space.' The pile of rubbish was alive, and not very friendly.

'Sorry,' Jamal said. 'I didn't realise.'

'Well, you do now. Go somewhere else.'

Jamal started paying more attention to the heaps of rubbish. They were all children, lying nose to tail next to the shops. Eventually Jamal saw a small gap between some squashed fruit boxes and a pile of grey rags. He poked the space carefully with his shoe, trying to decide if it was really empty.

'It's all right,' a girl's voice said. 'I was keeping that space for my friend.'

'I'm sorry. I'll find somewhere else.'

'I said it's all right. It's late – she'd be here by now if she was coming. You sleep there.'

Jamal thanked her and put his bag on the floor, his head towards the road. He would have preferred to have his head safely by the wall but the girl was lying that way. He wrapped the bag around him, pleased he could finally stop walking.

'She didn't come last night either, so it can be your space now.'

Jamal went to sleep wondering about the girl whose space he had taken and hoping that she was OK.

When he woke up everyone else was already moving, folding up their bedding and putting it together in piles then tying the piles with string.

'Come on! We've got to move. We've got to be out of here before the shops open.'

Jamal picked up his bag and looked at his feet. They were red and sore where his shoes had rubbed the skin. He decided to leave his shoes in the bag, with his book and the sheet that he'd taken from the laundry cart.

'Hurry up. If we're quick we can get down to where the nuns give out breakfast, but we'll have to run.'

'No, I can't go.'

'Why, are you fasting?' The girl sounded surprised.

'No, it's not that. It's just I was meant to go there ... to the orphanage, with the nuns. They'll know and keep me in.'

'Did you run away from the orphanage? That was stupid; they make a good breakfast.'

'No, I didn't want to go, so I ran away from the hospital.'

'Then why are you worried? They never saw you, so just don't tell them. Now come on or we won't get anything.'

Jamal started to follow her then realised that they were heading off the main road. He hesitated – he was hungry and he wanted breakfast, but he didn't want to get lost again.

'Come on! I'm not waiting. You'll be fine. They haven't got room for all the street kids. They aren't going to invite you to stay.'

Jamal made up his mind. He wanted breakfast.

He was pleased that he was able to get some food. He was almost sorry that he hadn't gone to the orphanage now, because the nuns seemed quite nice, not the monsters that Afiba had said they would be. But it was too late. Jamal wondered if the soldiers had found his grandfather. He hoped they hadn't. Jamal wanted to laugh when he thought how cross Grandfather would be if he came all the way to the city just to be sent home again. Yes, he thought, it would have been funny to see his grandfather – very very cross but afraid of the soldiers so having to pretend not to mind.

By the time Jamal got back to the main road he had finally stopped laughing – well, almost. He was still smiling as he turned away from the city and started to look for the ghosts again.

Following Your Nose

As Jamal headed further from the city, the road began to bend more often. At one point he wasn't sure if he was on the right course: the main road seemed to turn to the right, whereas the route Jamal was taking was unswerving but more like a track. But he remembered that the boy in the football shirt had told him to keep going straight, even if there were better roads, so that's what he did. Jamal walked along the track hoping he was still heading south. It was more difficult to tell which way he was going because there was so much smoke in the air ahead of him. He started to cough. It was the sort of smoke that came from a generator, but it didn't smell the same. Jamal couldn't believe this, but it seemed as if it smelt of fish. What sort of smoke smelt of fish? Not the smoke that the ghosts left behind, Jamal was sure of that.

As he got closer, his eyes started to sting. He thought that maybe there were huts ahead of him, but he wasn't sure. The huts seemed to be moving, but it was so hard to see. He kept walking, trying to make sense of the moving houses and the fishy smoke. The boys had been right – this place did smell awful. But it didn't smell of death; it smelt of fire and fish.

As he got closer he realised that the huts really *were* moving. They weren't huts; they were boats. Were the huts boats? Or were the boats huts? Jamal wasn't sure which. He hadn't seen any boats like these before. A few seemed like normal boats but there were others that were like houses, with washing lines strung between them, and smoke seeping through the roofs. It looked as if the huts – or boats – were on fire, but they weren't. They couldn't have been because people were going in and out of them, jumping from one boat to another. It was as if the city had grown too big so someone had said, 'Let's just build another one on the water.'

Jamal didn't think he would ever get used to living in the city. But he didn't think he could go back to the country either. He would miss the noise and the nights that were like days and the music and the people and the way the houses all leant on each other. He would miss everything.

The road suddenly bent round to the left, following the coast and heading away from the floating city. There were boats here too, but they were pulled out of the water. The beach was covered in old plastic bags and empty oil cans and fraying fishing-nets and every boat had a gaping hole in the side. What had happened? Jamal couldn't think of any reason why so many boats were being kept when they couldn't be used. Why didn't people break them up for firewood? It wasn't as if they didn't have fires: he had seen the smoke and the fires in the floating city.

He had just started to climb over the wall that kept the land and the sea apart when he smelt something familiar. That nutmeg scent that told him that the spirits were near. He slipped down the wall and away from the road, hoping that he could stay hidden, at least for a while. He was only just in time. The hissing whispering noises got louder and lights filled his eyes and the spirits rolled him on the rubbish-filled beach.

When he woke up his mouth was full of blood and sand. He wasn't sure which was worse. He knew that the spirits often bit his tongue, but he'd forgotten how much it hurt. All the time he was in the hospital the spirits had stayed away, but now they were back and Jamal was unhappy. He wondered if there was a way to tell them that they weren't welcome any more. When his family was alive it had been OK. He didn't mind if he was keeping the people he loved safe. But not now. There was no one left, only Jamal, so it was time they left him alone.

He spat the blood out of his mouth and climbed back over the wall. He'd been lucky; no one had noticed him. He would be able to continue his trek without anyone calling him names or throwing stones at him. All in all, not bad – definitely worth a mouthful of sand. He could hardly smell the smoke now; there was another smell on the air – not very strong but not very pleasant either. In fact, it almost made him want to smell the fish smoke again. The further he walked, the stronger the smell became. Jamal knew what the smell was: it was the smell that came when something was dead. Judging by how strong the smell was, something very big had been dead for a long time. He leant over the wall again, and threw up. He wanted to turn around, to go back to the smoke. But he remembered what the boys had told him. 'Follow your nose,' they had said: 'the road smells of death'. This must be the right road.

He spat the bad taste out of his mouth and started walking again. The road began to turn away from the sea.

Somewhere to Live

The air was full of flies as Jamal walked on. Not the normal summer flies; these were larger and angrier. Six months ago he would have run away. Gone somewhere that smelt sweeter, somewhere where there was less smoke, where the wind blew from the sea. But now it was OK. Jamal had become used to air that wasn't fresh – and as for the flies, at least they were alive. So he kept walking along the road, batting the flies away from his face as he went.

He walked long into the afternoon, and although he was passed by lots of lorries and quite a few pick-ups, there were no people walking with him. Maybe the road went nowhere, or maybe it was a bad road to follow. The road was too dry for Jamal to see many tracks, though he knew there would be wild dogs looking for food and men who would steal from anyone passing.

But he wasn't bothered. He had no food so the dogs would leave him alone. He had nothing left to steal so the robbers wouldn't bother with him either. He only had his book and he didn't think anyone would want that.

The book was filled with beautiful patterns but he knew this would not interest the thieves – thieves only wanted things they could sell. He opened the book and ran his hands across the pages.

'Like butterflies,' he said. 'A book of handkerchief butterflies that never die.'

Jamal felt sad as he thought of all the dead butterflies he'd seen when he left the mountain. He didn't feel sad about leaving his grandfather – he was quite pleased to have left him behind. Jamal had wanted his grandfather to be wise and kind. Like the grandfathers in the stories he had heard when he hid behind the thorn hedge. The stories that his uncles wove from the evening smoke. He would have been sad to leave a grandfather like that, but he didn't mind leaving the old man on the mountain.

He turned the pages of his book which fluttered and fell. They felt magical and were full of complicated patterns, meaningless but special because they reminded him of home. Maybe the old man hadn't been his grandfather after all. Maybe he was just waiting in his grandfather's cave, taking care of his things. Or maybe he was a thief, stealing Grandfather's food while he was out. Jamal decided that that was probably what had happened. If the old man was a thief, then he would have wanted Jamal to leave. That was why he was such a bad man. Jamal wished he'd realised this before. He could have waited for his grandfather to return and help him chase the thief away. But he had let his grandfather down. The thief had chased Jamal away instead; chased him down the mountain. And now his grandfather would never find him and the thief would have taken all the food from the cave. *Yes,* thought Jamal, *I really am unlucky after all. That's why I'll never be welcome anywhere.*

He looked at his book again, at the patterns curling across the page. They reminded him of the marks on the side of the red canister that the ghosts had left. They weren't the same, but they felt the same – as if they shared the same sort of magic. He traced his finger along a line of the black pictures. *These,* he thought, *could be pictures of fish leaping out of the water.* Sometimes there were dots and flicks above the fish. *Those are the flies that the fish want to catch. This is a good book; it is full of stories. And if I try to understand them they will be like the pictures on the ghost canister and they will tell me what to do next.*

So Jamal looked at the patterns of fish swimming through his book and decided that they were swimming towards the sunset. Then, before he could put the book away, thump! A mango hit him on the shoulder. He caught it before it fell on the ground. He closed the book and ate the mango.

He noticed that under the leaves there were lots of mangoes – small hard mangoes that were bruised and pecked. Jamal picked up as many as he could, dusting off the mud and the bugs before putting them in his bag. He didn't know how far he would have to walk so he tried to fill his bag. Mangoes were good to eat at any time – even if they were not quite ripe. When he'd gathered all the fruit, he tucked his book under his arm and started walking west, towards the sun. *I'm definitely going the right way,* he thought – the smell was getting stronger. He felt happy at last; he was sure that he would soon know what to do.

By the time Jamal got to the end of the road it was night. Ahead of him were fires, so many fires that he couldn't count them. More fires than he had fingers, probably more fires than mangoes. They rose in lines, marching up the hill like the army-worms that trooped up the trees before the big rains. The smell of rubbish was very strong here. So strong that he felt his stomach rising into his mouth. This was not a good place to be. Jamal couldn't hear any ghosts, or see them dancing in the fires, but somehow he was sure they were here. He couldn't see anyone around, but he knew he was being watched. He was just trying to decide if he should go closer to the fires or leave and come back in the morning when a heavy hand stung his ear.

'Hey you, boy. What do you want here?'

He still couldn't see anyone – it was too dark, the air too full of shapes and shadows – but he could smell the man, unwashed and drunk.

'Sorry, sir, I'm following the ghosts, sir. I'm going to the fires, sir, till it's morning.'

The heavy hand stung his ear again.

'And have you got a dash for Uncle, boy? So he can buy a little coffee and maybe look the other way while you sneak in where you're not meant to be?' The man separated himself from the shadows and leant over Jamal. He didn't smell of coffee. In fact, Jamal couldn't smell coffee at all, just the man and the sweet smell of nutmeg. Gradually all the other smells faded as the nutmeg breath of the spirits floated towards him. Jamal tried to ignore it.

'I've got nothing, sir. No coffee, no money for coffee. I've come for the spirits. I can keep them from you, sir.'

'Don't be stupid, boy.' Jamal felt his face sting as the man hit him again. 'None of your ignorant bush nonsense here. There are no spirits, no ghosts, no juju. This is a good Christian place. Just find a little dash for your uncle and you can go by the fire.'

Jamal didn't answer the man. The spirits were whispering buzzy little secrets and he could feel their smoky blackness flowing over him.

Although he didn't know it, Jamal fell to the ground, shaking at the watchman's feet.

The watchman – who did believe in spirits and ghosts after all – dropped his cigarette and ran back into the shadows. He forgot about his bribe, and about keeping people away from the rubbish – he just wanted to be away from Jamal and whatever was tormenting him.

When the spirits finally left Jamal, a boy was standing over him. He was a bit smaller than Jamal but looked much stronger.

'You feeling better?' He peered into Jamal's face. 'I'm Mham. I think it's short for something but I don't know what, 'cause it's so long since my mum was around to call my name. What are you called?'

'Jamal. That's my whole name, not short for anything.' Jamal sat up, checking the spirits hadn't bitten him or rolled him into a fire. He felt fine so he looked for his book and his bag. The bag was gone.

'I've got your mangoes. Didn't want you to spoil them. I ate a couple, though. Hope that's OK. You did well to keep them from Johnson. He was so scared of you – it made me laugh. Here.' Mham held out his hand and pulled Jamal to his feet. 'Come on, this way.'

And that was it. Jamal moved into Mham's hut and learnt to pick and sort the rubbish. The watchman stayed away from them, so they didn't have to pay him a bribe, but he wasn't the only one who expected a share of their money. They paid one man for the right to stay in the hut, another for the right to sell plastic, another so that they could use the water tap by the gate, and someone else so their stuff didn't get stolen when they were working on the dump.

They might have starved, but they didn't. When they found plastic bottles, they tied them together and sold them to the men in trucks. When they found wood, they collected it and dragged it back to their hut to burn. When they found clothes, they would either wear them or sell them to the rag man. When they found food, they would take it into the hut and eat it. But they had other ways to survive too. Jamal would sometimes walk back to the bush and collect fruit while Mham stayed behind on the dump. It was always Jamal who went for the fruit because the watchman was afraid of him and let him through the gate without paying.

When the rains came there were more accidents. The water made the piles of rubbish unstable. There were landslides and mudslides. The fires wouldn't light and the huts leaked. But no one left the dump – there was nowhere else to go. They made hats from carrier bags and capes from fertilizer sacks so they could keep working. There were no more mangoes because all the fruit rotted. Jamal tried using a bucket of water to catch termites like his aunties used to do. But it didn't work. They caught flies and once they found a fat mouse drowned in the bucket, but nothing they could eat. It was a difficult time. Somehow, the boys managed to make enough money to survive, although Mham developed a cough and the cuts on Jamal's hands and feet became infected. The boys were pleased when the clouds rolled away and took the rains with them – everyone was. The rubbish on the dump began to dry out and life got a little easier.

In the evening the boys would sometimes go from the dump and walk to the sea. Not often because it was risky to leave the hut. There was always someone who wanted a new roof or some tin sheet, and an unattended hut could be raided for materials

– particularly if it only belonged to small boys. But it was cooler by the sea and there were people and music. And when people were enjoying themselves there was often food to be stolen.

'So what happened to your mum?' Jamal asked, passing Mham the bag of crisps that he'd 'found' by someone's icebox.

'She got buried.'

'Eh?' *Well, everyone gets buried,* Jamal thought, *after they're dead.*

'It was a big slide – on the old part of the dump. It was in the morning. We were all picking together – me, my brothers, and mum with my baby sister. Our bag blew away and I went after it. The rubbish just shifted. I thought we wouldn't find them – wish we hadn't in some ways. Should have left them. You don't want to see them after. Remember that, Jamal: if I go under, leave me there.'

They sat in silence for awhile – Mham remembering his family and Jamal thinking that he wouldn't leave his friend under a landslide, no matter what he said.

'So,' said Mham. 'What about your mum? What happened to her?'

'She turned yellow and died,' Jamal said. 'Not straight away. She was sick first and got a fever. But she just got worse, then her eyes and her hands went all yellow and she died. It was OK till she died. I wasn't alone.'

'Yeah,' Mham said. 'It's being alone, isn't it?' Then he said, 'But we're OK now, aren't we? You and me.'

'Yeah, we're OK,' Jamal said, not really meaning it. He dropped the empty crisp packet – it wasn't worth anything – and started to climb over the sea wall. 'You coming?' he asked Mham.

They walked home in silence.

A Way of Life

The dump was like a small town – everything that happened in a town happened in the dump. People died and babies were born. Young people fell in love and teenagers argued with their parents. It was just that all these things happened surrounded by rubbish. None of the children went to school, but that didn't bother Jamal – he had never been to school anyway. He was just happy to fit in. He and Mham made a good team. Mham watched out for Jamal when the spirits came and Jamal earned extra money that they could use to buy food in the market.

Once every month, more or less, people came from the government. From the sanitation department. They always said the same thing. They said they were going to close the dump. That they were going to build a new recycling centre on the other side of town. They told the rubbish pickers that they would have to leave. They said they would tear down their huts and – if they didn't move on – they would put them in jail. They didn't mean it. But Jamal didn't know this.

The first time Jamal saw them with their security guards and their pieces of paper he ran to find Mham.

'Mham, quick! Men have come to close the dump. They're at the gate, they say we must leave. Where will we go, Mham? What will we do?'

Mham was searching for aluminium cans in the back of a truck, trying to get the best rubbish before anyone else arrived. He looked up when he heard Jamal shouting.

'Look at this, Jamal. This lot must have come from a restaurant or something. It's full of cans.' He lifted up a plastic bag full of Coke cans. 'There's tons more. Come up and help me.'

'It's too late. We've got to go. The men ... they're going to send us all to jail. Mham, what will we do?'

'Chill, friend. It's nothing. Good job I found this though. We'll need the extra cash. Now come up and help. We need to get all the cans before anyone else gets here.'

'But the men ... the gate ... jail.'

'It's nothing, Jamal. Really, it's nothing. They aren't going to build a recycling centre because that would cost too much – and they've already spent all the money.'

Jamal looked at his friend. He had definitely heard the men saying that they were going to close the dump. Close the dump and send everyone to jail.

'They won't close the dump either. Just think about it, Jamal. Where would all this rubbish go if they closed the dump? People won't stop throwing stuff away. It has to go somewhere and nobody else wants it. Just us. So climb up here and help me get these tins. We'll all club together and, if we've got enough, they'll leave us alone.'

'And if we haven't got enough?' Jamal was still worried.

'Then someone will go to jail – and stay there till we raise the cash. But don't worry. We all chip in. Everyone gives what they've got saved. Even the mean ones. We're all family here, Jamal. We have to be.'

Mham was right. The men didn't really want to close the dump. They didn't really want the bother of sending anyone to jail either. They just wanted some extra money. They got money from the men who drove the garbage trucks and money from the rubbish pickers and a salary from the government. It wasn't fair, but it was what they did. And – because they expected life to be unfair – the people on the dump paid up every month.

Mham was right about the dump being like a family, too. There were people who would give you a meal if you were hungry and people who were mean to everyone. The trick was to make yourself useful, to have a special skill that people needed.

The rubbish pickers all knew that Jamal attracted evil spirits. That was his special skill. They would pay him to take the spirits from the sick, or to distract the spirits so they didn't notice a wedding, or a new baby.

Mham and Jamal had lots of ways to get by – and not all of them were strictly legal. Some weeks they made enough money and some weeks they didn't. But they worked together and somehow they never quite starved. They often went to bed hungry, though.

Jamal missed his home and his comfortable life, but that home felt a long way away. Often when he talked about home he wasn't sure if he was talking about his old home or his new home with Mham. He felt safe with the rubbish pickers; he'd even stopped looking for the ghosts. Some days he almost forgot about them altogether, but they hadn't forgotten about him. They still had plans for his future.

The Return of the Ghosts

J amal got used to feeling hungry but he was never really used to being dirty. He would run his hand over his head and try to catch whatever was crawling there. He remembered when the nurse had taken him to the barber's stall and how smooth and clean his head had felt. It made him wish that he'd stolen some soap when he left the hospital, but he knew it wouldn't have helped much. Water was too expensive for the boys to waste it washing themselves. So most of the time Jamal had dirt under his nails and dirt between his toes and dirt just about anywhere that could be dirty. It made his skin itch and it made people avoid him when he left the dump.

He was sitting on a box, picking at the scabs that formed whenever he cut himself on the broken glass that people threw away, when he remembered why he had come to the dump. He had been looking for clues to help him understand the pictures on the ghost cylinders but he'd almost forgotten about the ghosts since he had met Mham.

'Hey, Jamal, any metal? Petey's down there; he's paying real cash today.'

Jamal looked at his friend before getting up and pushing a pole into the ground. He listened for the sound of metal hitting metal.

'Yup, come up and help. This sounds heavy.'

Mham scrambled across the fresh pile of trash, happy to dig if it meant having real cash they could spend at real food stalls. The boys worked together, soon filling the sack that Mham had brought up the hill, but it was all small, light stuff. That made the sack easier to carry, though it was worth less to the boys. Petey paid by the pound so they really wanted to reach the heavy lump of metal that Jamal had heard. They wanted to get to it quickly too, before any of the other pickers noticed.

'Got it!' shouted Mham. 'Don't know what it is though. I've not seen anything like this before. What do you think, Jamal? Jamal?' He looked round but Jamal had stopped digging.

'They're back,' he said, very quietly. 'They've found me. I was meant to be finding them, trying to put things right, but I'd forgotten.' He stared, not at Mham but at the red cylinder he was holding.

'Good! Keep forgetting about them and help me with this. We've got to get it down to Petey before he goes.'

'No! No, Mham, we can't take it to Petey. It's like the one I left at Grandfather's, like the ones the ghosts left when they killed everyone. Look at the pictures, Mham. Look at them. What do they mean?'

Mham shook his head. He needed the canister to make up the weight in the sack, but he could see that Jamal wasn't going to let him sell it, not yet. *Maybe,* he thought, *we could sell the other stuff now and keep the cylinder till next time.* Maybe Jamal would have got over whatever was bothering him by then.

'Look, I've got to get this stuff to Petey before he goes. You take the cylinder back to the hut and wait there. Don't tell anyone you've got it. They'll take it if you do. We need the money, Jamal. Do you understand? Keep it a secret.' He wrapped the cylinder in a shirt that he'd picked up and handed it to Jamal.

'Keep it hidden, remember. I'll be back – soon as I can. Hide it. We'll decide what to do when I get back.' Then he took the metal rod from Jamal and raced down to the gate where Petey was weighing sacks and arguing over prices.

Jamal hurried to their hut. He needed to hurry: the canister had reminded him of the ghosts and remembering them had called the spirits. Already the smell of the dump was being hidden by the smell of nutmeg. He needed to be in the hut before the spirits breathed on him. Even if the other pickers were afraid of him, they would still try to steal the cylinder if he dropped it. So Jamal ran down the rubbish heap to Mham's hut. He just had time to hide the cylinder under his bed before the world around him disappeared and he fell to the ground. But the spirits didn't stay long. He was awake, but shaky when Mham came in, holding a handful of copper coins.

'Hot food tonight.' He grinned.

Jamal grinned too; they hadn't been to the market for ages.

'We have to look at this first,' he said. 'Look at the marks. What story are they trying to tell?'

They both looked hard at the patterns on the cylinder. They weren't very clear – the cylinder was scratched and dented – but they could make out most of them.

'The pictures definitely make a story,' Mham said. 'Look! I think it goes like this: one drop of water fell on a tree, but the tree was magic and it didn't need water so the leaves fell off. The magic leaves fell on the fish and freed them from a net. Then the fish swam through the river to the graveyard and the magic made the bones smile. Finally, a man caught a drop of the water in his hand and it made his eyes grow large and his nose grow long and he turned into a dog.'

'It's a very good story, Mham, but I don't think it can be the right story. It doesn't explain the ghosts or why they killed all the animals and all the people when they came. It doesn't say what we have to do. All stories tell you something. Yours was a good story, but it didn't tell us what to do.'

'What about the rest of it? The writing, I mean. Can you read the writing, Jamal? I can't. Mum couldn't afford the uniform so I didn't go to school. How about you, Jamal? Did you go to school?'

Jamal shook his head.

'Can anyone here read?'

'Some, I guess, but they'll want us to pay a dash before they do. If we pay them we won't have enough left to go to Mama Green and get some chicken.'

The boys looked at the words on the cylinder and the coins next to it.

'Let's get some chicken,' said Jamal.

'Yes, and we'll take the story tube with us. Maybe we'll think better when our bellies are full.'

Jamal fetched his book – he never forgot it when he left the dump. Then they wrapped the cylinder in a cloth and set out for the market. The chicken was good and they would have liked more, but Mama Green didn't give her food away for free and they had spent most of their money.

'Just enough left for a Fanta,' Mham said, and they headed to a row of stalls where someone had a cooler full of drinks. Mham handed over the last of their money and offered the bottle to his friend. Jamal shook his head. Suddenly he thought of the people at the bottom of the mountain and the drinks he'd taken from the icebox. He didn't want the sweet drink after all.

A heavy hand landed on Jamal's shoulder.

'You don't like orange drinks, boy?' the man said. 'That's very strange.'

Jamal tried to run – Mham had already disappeared. They both thought the same thing. They thought the man was going to say they were thieves.

'I see your friend has left you. What will you do now?'

Jamal wanted to say that he would go home, but the man was pushing him away from the market and he felt frightened. He tried to wriggle free and nearly got away, but he dropped his book and had to stop. He couldn't leave his book. He bent to pick it up but the old man was already holding it. *He's very quick for such an old man,* Jamal thought.

'Where did you get this from, boy? Who did you steal it from? Tell me now, don't lie. This is an expensive book. Who did you steal it from?' The old man sounded even more unfriendly now. He sounded scary. *Like the voice of God,* thought Jamal. It was a voice you had to listen to.

'No, sir. I didn't steal it. It's my book, sir. I brought it with me, from home. The Imam gave it to me. He said I should always keep it, sir. Please give it back, sir. It is my book, sir.'

'Do you know what this book is, boy?'

'No, sir. But it is a beautiful book, sir. Full of beautiful patterns, sir. I like to look at it. It *is* my book, sir. Please may I have it back?'

'It *is* a beautiful book, boy, and you ought to learn the words. Would you like to learn the words, boy? To study the words in the book and to have plenty to eat and a bed to sleep in? Would you like that, boy? I'm sure you would like a bath, wouldn't you? Come on, this way. Let us get you clean and washed and you can start your lessons with the other boys in the morning.'

Jamal wished that Mham was still with him. Mham would have known what to do. He would know if they should trust this man. But Mham wasn't there and the man did not seem so bad after all and Jamal really,

really wanted a bath. The man also had Jamal's book and he didn't want to lose it.

'Come on now, boy. Don't worry about your clothes, we'll get you new ones when we get to the school.'

Jamal wondered what clothes the man was talking about – then he realised. He was carrying the cylinder – still wrapped in the old shirt – under his arm.

The man must think I've got a change of clothes! Jamal laughed to himself. *If I had a spare set of clothes,* he thought, *I'd sell them and buy some more chicken.*

Jamal decided to follow the man. Mham was left hiding in the market.

School

J amal kept looking around for Mham but the man pushed him forwards, away from the market and the places he knew. They turned left then right then left again, until Jamal had no idea where he was. Eventually they reached a black metal gate set into a high white wall. Had it taken them fifteen minutes to get there or was it fifty? Jamal couldn't be sure. The man had talked so much and walked so fast and turned so often that they might be in the next town or they might have doubled back to the market. Jamal was too confused to think.

'Here we are, boy. Now you can stop being an urchin and learn to be a man of God. Come, let's get you clean.'

Jamal said nothing. He didn't know what he was expected to say. The compound was enormous: his uncles' compound, all the huts and the animal pens, the thorn fence and even his own hut and the meeting tree, they would all have fitted inside this compound. But there were no animals, no huts, no meeting tree, just a plain swept yard surrounded by long, low buildings. Jamal couldn't think why so many buildings would be in one compound. He couldn't think how they could feed all the people who must live here if there were no animals. He couldn't think how they settled arguments if there was no meeting tree. He couldn't think at all.

'Ahmed, over here. Take young … What's your name, boy? Take him to the showers and get him clean and find him some clean clothes.'

The man didn't wait for Jamal to answer; he just wandered off and left Jamal with Ahmed, a tall boy, or maybe a young man who hadn't worked hard enough to build his muscles. Jamal felt lost. It didn't seem very long ago that every day had been the same, and now everything kept changing. He wanted his old life back, but he didn't seem to be getting any closer to finding the ghosts.

'Come on. The showers will be hot now. Not like in the morning – they're cold then. What's your name? Where are your parents? Mine sent me here – did yours? How old are you?'

Jamal decided that Ahmed was definitely still a boy. He didn't talk like a man. Men saved words like water, only asking what needed answers, but Ahmed couldn't stop asking questions.

'I'll leave you. There's soap – do you like the smell? I do. I'll get a towel and some clothes. How big are you? Smaller than me, definitely, but bigger than Jo. I'll find something. I'll be back. See you!'

Jamal undressed, leaving his clothes on a bench with the cylinder. Then he stood under the shower until the smell from the dump ran from him and his skin stopped itching. He thought he'd found the only place in the city that was quiet. Then Ahmed bounced back into the room with the clean clothes.

'I've got your towel. It's a bit thin but it's OK, really. They're all a bit thin to be honest, but you get used to them. Here's the clothes – same as mine. We all wear the same here. Hope they're the right size.'

How did he do it? Jamal felt short of breath just listening.

'Wow! What's this? Where did you get it? Look what it says! Did you read it?'

Jamal was about to say that he couldn't read when Ahmed started to sound out the letters:

ung corp. item 174568. RICIN formula 74. US nufacture.
Danger to life.

Safe we must be worn. Respirators must be worn.
Avoid contact with sin wash im ly.
Envir m tl pollutant.

Ahmed looked confused.

'These words don't make sense – well, not all of them. Why have you got this? It looks dangerous. Don't touch it – I'll get help.'

Ahmed dashed from the shower room, shouting as he went.

Jamal didn't understand what the fuss was about. It wasn't dangerous – not now, not now the ghosts had gone. He finished drying himself then pulled on the clothes that Ahmed had left. They felt strange and heavy on his shoulders, but they were clean and it was good not to be dirty any more.

The man from the market pushed through the shower room door. Sweat dripped down his nose and he was panting as he leant against the wall.

'Where did you get this? Why have you brought it here?'

Jamal had never seen anyone look so angry.

'We found it in the dump, sir. We wanted to know what it said. No one at the dump could read it, sir. We just wanted to know what it said.' Jamal was about to explain about the ghosts but the man from the market had already started to calm down and was suddenly talking in a soothing voice.

'Ah, you found it, did you? You didn't know what it was? Well, I'm pleased you brought it to me. I will get rid of it, safely. It is good that you brought it here.' He held out his hand towards Jamal. 'Come, boys, let us talk.'

Jamal was confused; the man's voice sounded reassuring now, but would he shout again if Jamal said the wrong thing?

Ahmed pushed him slightly. 'We'd better go,' he said.

That worried Jamal even more. Ahmed had become quieter, almost normal. The man kept smiling as he led them to his office. Jamal didn't like his smile; it didn't look quite right. It wasn't a happy smile, or a kind smile. It was the sort of smile that said 'I wish you hadn't come to visit today as we have no food to give you,' when your voice was saying, 'Uncle, it is good that you and your family have come to see us.'

But no one was visiting, so Jamal wondered what the man was trying to hide.

'Now, boys, I will tell you about that thing that you brought here. It is a wicked thing. The soldiers use it to kill people. It comes from the Americans. This thing you have found is very wicked and it is the soldiers who own it and it is very bad.'

Jamal knew it was bad – he had seen the ghosts snaking out of the cylinders in his compound and he had seen what they had done to the people on the mountain. But he had never seen any soldiers near the cylinders, only ghosts. He had seen soldiers in the hospital, but there had been no ghosts there. There had been the strange drink that had made him sleepy, but definitely no ghosts. He hadn't seen any Americans either, or any government officials. Why was the man from the market saying these things?

'The soldiers will come and beat you if they think you have stolen this thing from them. Do you understand?'

Ahmed nodded and Jamal nodded too. But he didn't really understand at all. Why would the soldiers have thrown the cylinder away if they wanted it? And if they wanted it then surely they would be glad if you told them you had found it?

'So neither of you boys should mention this thing to anyone. No one but us should know about it. Do you understand?'

Ahmed nodded his head but Jamal did not.

'But my friend, he has seen it. He helped me carry it, sir.'

The man put his hands together and looked over them at the boys.

'But your friend does not know what this thing is, does he?' Jamal shook his head. 'And your friend is only a dirty scavenger so no one will believe what he says.'

Jamal didn't think that was true but he didn't think that the man from the market would listen to anyone.

'What about my grandfather?' Jamal asked. 'He saw the one I found by the mountain. He saw it and he threw it at me, sir.'

The man shook his head again.

'No, it was not the same. It was another sort of thing, not the same at all.'

Jamal was about to explain but Ahmed kicked him hard so he just nodded.

The man from the market looked pleased. He handed the boys a bottle of Sprite and opened another for himself.

'You must be thirsty after all this excitement. You can share that, but finish it before you get to the dormitory or all the boys will want to find dangerous things.'

The man took a drink from the bottle and then laughed, dribbles of Sprite and spit sticking to his beard. Jamal didn't like the way he laughed. It wasn't the sort of laugh that followed a joke, more the sort that came before rotten fruit was thrown at a beggar. Jamal nodded to himself; this man was definitely the sort of person who would throw things at beggars, or at boys who were troubled by spirits.

'Good, good. I'm pleased you understand. Now go to the dormitory, boys. It's time for your beds.' The boys got up to go. As they reached the door the man said: 'Goodnight, boys. Now remember, don't talk about this. Don't talk about this at all.'

A Bed in the Dormitory

J amal followed Ahmed as he raced outside and then sat down on the steps outside a long, low building. Ahmed had opened the Sprite and had already taken three or four gulps before Jamal reached him. Ahmed passed the bottle to his new friend but Jamal shook his head. He didn't trust the man from the market.

There was another reason why Jamal didn't want a drink. While Ahmed was drinking he finally stopped talking. Jamal still missed his hut at home, where the only sounds had been the animals outside and his uncles telling stories in the compound. He was not used to so much noise. Even Mham didn't talk as much as Ahmed did, and Jamal had thought that Mham talked too much.

'What happened there?' Ahmed asked. 'We usually drink water, now we've got this.' He waved the half-empty bottle towards Jamal. 'We haven't got to share it with the other boys. Here, have a turn – I can't drink it all. Well, I could, but it wouldn't be fair. You got it really – you found the cylinder.'

Ahmed stopped talking while he had another drink.

'You got him worried. Where did you really find it? What is it for?'

Ahmed went on and on. Question after question, only stopping when he drank Sprite from the bottle. Jamal wanted to shut out the noise but Ahmed just kept talking. Eventually the drink was finished and Ahmed got up.

'C'mon, let's get to bed. Got to be up early.'

They went into a room where a dozen boys jeered and shouted, complaining about being disturbed and calling Ahmed names. Jamal waited for someone to throw fruit at them, or worse, but nothing came their way. Ahmed pointed to a bed at the end of the room.

'Better take that one. It used to be Joseph's but he left – not sure where he went.'

There were a few shouted comments about Joseph and why his bed was empty until Ahmed threw the empty Sprite bottle at one of the boys and they all forgot about Joseph. They all wanted to know how Ahmed had got the drink. Some thought that he'd just picked up an empty bottle; others thought he'd stolen it. Ahmed was happy to be the centre of attention.

Jamal crawled into the bed. It was not very comfortable. It was too springy and it rocked and squeaked with every movement. At home, Jamal slept on old blankets piled on the floor. At the dump he slept next to Mham on a mattress that they had dragged into their hut. Jamal wondered if he could pull the mattress off the squeaky frame and onto the floor, but there were too many people in the room. Someone would notice and then everyone would laugh at him. Jamal decided that it was better to lie awake, trying not to move, and work out how to get back to the dump and to Mham.

He wanted to stay awake. He tried to stay awake. But eventually he fell asleep. He was sound asleep when Ahmed pushed him out of bed.

'C'mon, we'll be late.'

The room seemed to be full of boys and it took Jamal a while to remember where he was and what was going on.

'Why is everyone rushing?' he asked. 'Is it time for breakfast?'

Ahmed laughed.

'Breakfast? Where have you been? It's time for prayers. Get a move on.'

It wasn't even light. Jamal couldn't believe that anyone would want to get up before dawn unless they had to. And why weren't they starting the day with breakfast? Jamal was used to getting up at dawn. He was used to waking up when the birds started singing and when the daytime insects started to move in the morning heat. But he was not used to getting up *before* dawn and he really wanted to go back to sleep. The day definitely ought to start with eating, but it was clear that wasn't going to happen.

Ahmed took Jamal to a room with benches that faced taps on the wall.

'We wash here,' said Ahmed.

Jamal looked around for soap and towels but couldn't see either.

Other boys were sitting on the benches and washing themselves in what Jamal thought was a very odd way.

Ahmed looked at Jamal. 'Don't you know how to wash before prayers?'

Jamal didn't say anything; he'd never been taught how to pray. He knew that his uncles said their prayers. He had seen the watchman at the hospital take his mat and go to pray, but he'd never actually seen anyone pray. He couldn't remember how often his uncles prayed – he thought it was three or maybe five times a day, but he couldn't be sure. He didn't even know that he was meant to wash before praying. And he certainly didn't know that he had to wash in a special way. Jamal was sure that everyone would notice and that they would chase him away with sticks.

'It's not fair. I haven't even had breakfast.'

Ahmed looked at Jamal and shook his head.

'The Imam was right; you are very odd. Just do what I do and you'll get breakfast later. It'll be OK, Jamal. Don't worry.'

So that's what Jamal did. He sat next to Ahmed and washed himself just like his new friend. Then he followed Ahmed as they went to pray with the other boys.

Ghosts and Honey Cakes

'Something's wrong,' said Jamal. 'Something feels wrong.'

Ahmed put his hand on Jamal's shoulder. 'I said don't worry. Just do the same as me. I'll teach you properly later.'

Jamal wanted to tell his new friend that he wasn't worried about the prayers, that he could feel something was wrong. He wanted to tell Ahmed that he could feel something bad in the air, something heading towards them. He didn't get the chance. Ahmed still had his arm around Jamal when the spirits discovered Jamal's new hiding place.

Jamal woke up in a very small room. It was cool and dark – somewhere Jamal hadn't been before. He could hear people talking outside the room. They were talking about him and not even whispering.

'He's possessed. We should beat it out of him.'

'No, he's ill. We should take him to a doctor.'

'That will be expensive. Let's beat it out of him.'

'No, it's our duty to take him to a doctor.'

'It's our duty to see he's cured. Let's beat it out of him.'

'No, he's ill. I will deal with it.'

'I'll fetch you a stick.'

Jamal recognised the voice of the man from the market. He remembered where he was and why he wanted to get back to the dump. He didn't like the man from the market and he didn't want anyone to beat him with a stick. Jamal wondered if now would be a good time to leave.

Ahmed came into the room and put his fingers to his lips.

'What happened? You just fell down, and then you were shaking. I've never seen anything like it. Has it happened before? They said it's "A Pill At Sea", but I didn't see you take any pills. Can you do it when you want to? And does it hurt? Oh, yes, and do you want some tea?'

Jamal started to laugh.

'Why did you tell me to be quiet, Ahmed? You never stop talking even for a minute.'

Ahmed started to laugh as well. He kept laughing until there were tears in his eyes.

When the Imam came into Jamal's room, Ahmed was sitting on Jamal's bed and laughing out loud.

They tried to stop when they saw the Imam, but that just made them laugh more.

'I see you've woken up and that you feel well enough for visitors.' The Imam looked at Ahmed. 'Maybe your visitor could go and get us all some tea while you and I talk.'

Ahmed got off the bed.

'Yes, sir,' he said, not meeting the Imam's eyes.

'And Ahmed, maybe you could ask Cook for a few honey cakes too. I'm sure Jamal is hungry.'

The Imam didn't say anything else until they heard Ahmed slam through the screen door on his way to the kitchen, but he looked at Jamal very carefully. Jamal wondered if he was deciding whether to wait for the stick or to just beat him with his fists. But eventually he smiled at Jamal.

'You look as if you've had a rough time. Have you always lived on the dump?'

Jamal didn't really want to say anything – not till he knew why he was being asked these questions. He thought about the questions the judge had asked and what the soldier had said about letting people think that he was simple. He had liked the soldier and trusted her, so he decided to pretend to be just a little bit simple now.

'So what about your parents? Do your mum or dad live on the dump?'

Jamal shook his head, hoping that there wouldn't be any more questions.

'Brothers? Sisters? Any other relatives? I hear there was a boy with you in the market. Was he your cousin?'

Jamal thought about his grandfather. Did he have to tell this man about Grandfather? It would be a lie to say that he had no relatives, but the old man might not have actually been his grandfather. Jamal wasn't sure and the old man hadn't seemed that sure either.

'Everyone died when the ghosts came.' Jamal thought that was a safe answer. It was very nearly true and the man hadn't actually asked about grandparents.

'Ghosts, eh? Do you want to tell me about them?'

Jamal felt happier with that question. No need to lie even a little bit. He didn't want to talk about the ghosts at all.

'Maybe later then. We need to get you to a doctor, to sort out your skin – it looks infected. And while we are there we'll see if we can find out about these fits.'

Jamal was surprised; he had expected more questions and more difficult questions. The man was being nice and Jamal didn't expect someone to be nice to him if he was going to beat him.

'So is this the first time you've had a fit?'

Jamal was silent.

'Not answering that, eh? How about this: did you know you were sick before you came here?'

Jamal nodded very slightly. He remembered the people by the factory calling him a witch. And the people in the dump had avoided him unless they had problems with spirits. Jamal didn't want this man to call him a witch.

'And did you have any medicine to stop you being sick?'

Another nod.

'I see. But you didn't bring any medicine with you. Why was that?'

Jamal nodded again. He was trying not to say too much but suddenly he wanted to tell this man about everything that had happened. He wanted to tell him about the ghosts and the people who had died and the soldiers and the nurse and the boys who slept on the street and about Mham and about the boy who stole his medicine. All the words that Jamal had been keeping hidden came tumbling out and he told the Imam everything, even about his grandfather.

Then Jamal cried. He was still crying when Ahmed brought the tea.

The Imam took the tea and the cakes and sent Ahmed back to the kitchens and let Jamal cry until he'd run out of tears. He didn't speak until Jamal had quite finished.

'Tea first, then cakes, and then a visit to the doctor. Everything else can wait till the morning.'

The Imam put his hand on Jamal's head, then pulled it away again, looking at his hand in surprise.

'A haircut before the doctor's, I think. Just so you're a bit more presentable. We don't want people thinking that we neglect you.' He took a white cloth from his pocket and wiped his hands before throwing the cloth in the bin.

'I'd like a haircut,' Jamal said. 'And I'd like another honey cake.'

A New Start

J amal sat on a stool in the middle of the compound. One of the older boys was standing over him holding a pair of electric clippers and looking at Jamal's almost bald head.

Jamal wanted him to finish because the noise of the clippers was stopping him listening to the two men talking by the gate. The Imam was arguing with the man from the market again. Jamal thought they were arguing about him.

'He's a troublemaker, believe me. I won't say why but I happen to know that he'll bring trouble.'

'Well, he doesn't look as if he could be that much trouble. There's hardly anything of him.'

'I'm not talking about him getting into fights; I'm talking about real trouble.'

They looked over to where the boy was rubbing some very smelly cream into Jamal's scalp.

'What sort of real trouble? The poor kid hasn't even been to school, so when do you think he's learnt to be trouble?'

'I could tell you things.'

'Fine! Tell me things, if there's anything to tell, but I don't think he'll be a problem. In fact, I think he could be quite bright. Poor kid just needs a chance.'

The man from the market threw an empty can at the wall. It bounced off and hit one of the smaller boys on the back of the head.

'Pick up the rubbish,' the man shouted.

Just like him not to say sorry, thought Jamal.

The Imam came over to Jamal.

'Phew, that smells bad. Still, it will keep your little friends away.' He nodded his head at the boy with the clippers. 'Good job. Make sure you use alcohol to clean the blades and put the clippings in the boiler.'

He held out his hand to Jamal.

'Come on, young man. We've got an appointment to keep.'

The Imam and Jamal left the compound and went into town. They visited the doctor, who asked Jamal about the medicine he had taken and how often he took it. Then he asked about the hospital with the soldiers. He looked at the scabs and cuts on Jamal's head and arms. Jamal was weighed and measured and poked and prodded then sent to sit outside while the doctor and the Imam were talking.

They came away with a bag full of medicines and creams. Then they went into town, to the market and a book shop, and to a shop that didn't seem to sell anything, and which the Imam called a bank. Jamal thought that banks were there to keep the water in the river but he couldn't see any water. It just looked like an ordinary building to him.

Jamal enjoyed his trip – and he particularly enjoyed the ice cream that the Imam bought when they left the doctor's house.

It wasn't a perfect day out, though, because Jamal felt as if he was being watched. He couldn't be sure but he thought he saw the man from the market talking to one of the nurses outside the doctor's house. And he wondered if the same man was sitting in a coffee shop close to where the Imam bought the ice cream. Finally, Jamal was almost sure he was talking to a man in dark clothes outside the bank. He asked the Imam if the man from the market had come to town too.

'Maybe. He's a busy man. Now, have you ever had a ride on a bus?'

Jamal didn't think they needed to go on the bus; they had walked into town and he thought they could have easily walked back again. But the Imam led Jamal to a crowd of people who were pushing to get on an old yellow bus. He'd never been on a bus before and he liked to do new things. He liked looking out of the window and he liked how the bus rattled and bumped as it went around corners. He even liked the way more and more people crowded on board, with two or sometimes three people on each seat. But he was pleased when they got back to the compound. He wanted to tell Ahmed about everything he'd done. But when he got back he didn't see Ahmed.

'The doctor said you must rest today,' the Imam told him. 'So stay in your room. After prayers we'll talk and I think I'll get Ahmed to sleep in your room in case you are ill in the night.'

Jamal lay down in the cool, quiet room and listened to the noises of the boys getting ready for prayers.

He must have fallen asleep because when he woke up he saw a jug of water by his bed that hadn't been there before. When he looked around he was surprised to see the man from the market standing by the door. Jamal decided not to drink any of the water, just in case the man from the market had put it there.

'I know you're a spy from the military,' the man said. 'I know where you came from and how you got the gas canister. I'm watching you and I'll make you pay.'

He turned round to leave Jamal's room but bumped into Ahmed who was running in with some lunch.

'Get out of my way.' He pushed past Ahmed, taking a piece of fried chicken from Jamal's plate as he did so.

'What did he want?'

'I'm not sure,' said Jamal. 'But I don't think he likes me.'

Ahmed shrugged.

'You and everyone else,' he said. 'Let's eat. Have you heard, I'm moving in here? And you get extra food until you're well. And you don't have to go to lessons. And, and … and I can't remember what else I was going to tell you.'

It took a while before the spirits stopped visiting Jamal. The doctor said that the medical staff were sorting his meds out. Some days Jamal just slept all day and other days he kept being sick, but eventually he learnt when to take the medicine and how much medicine to take and people stopped noticing that he was different. He moved back into the dormitory and Ahmed taught him the right order in which to wash himself and the words to say when he was washing. He began to feel at home. Everything would have been fine if it wasn't for the man from the market.

*

Jamal was excused early prayers for another month – until the doctor decided that he was well enough to cope. And he didn't have to fast during Ramadan – even though everyone else did. It made him feel bad when he went to the kitchen for bread or tea. But when he tried to miss meals – like the other boys – the Imam would find him and make him eat. Ahmed said that he should miss out on the evening meal if he didn't have to fast, but he was only joking. No one seemed to mind that Jamal was different. No one called him a witch, or said that he was cursed. No one was afraid of him. He was just another boy in a school full of boys. He was in a class with the small boys, but that was because he had started school later than everyone else. He was even making friends. Ahmed was still his best friend, though.

Ahmed and Jamal would often go into town after Friday prayers. It was the only day when they didn't have lessons. Sometimes they would watch the other boys playing football in the park – they would only watch because Jamal was really bad at football. He often forgot which team he was on and would pass the ball to the wrong person – or kick it into the wrong goal. At other times they would walk to the market – just to look around. The boys didn't have any money – none of the students did – and Jamal had stopped stealing. But they went to the market anyway. Jamal wanted to find Mham and maybe bring him back to the school. He thought that Mham would like the school and would appreciate having clean clothes and plenty to eat. He didn't tell Ahmed that he was looking for Mham – he didn't tell anyone – but he kept looking. Mham was never there. But Jamal was sure that someone else was. He was sure that the man from the market was following him.

Mham was also looking for Jamal. He asked people in the market and people at the dump. He looked around the town, working out from the market, looking for places where Jamal might have gone. But he couldn't go to town very often – it was harder to make enough money without Jamal to help. He missed his friend.

A Different Destiny

J amal was sitting alone in the common room. The other boys had finished their homework but Jamal was still catching up. He could read Arabic and English now but his writing was still dreadful. He wanted to fill the page with the patterns of leaping fish that he'd first seen in the Qur'an before the words meant anything to him. The problem was his writing looked as if it was made by a lizard with ink on its tail. More than anything else – even more than learning the Qur'an by heart or understanding long division – Jamal longed to have beautiful handwriting, so he spent almost every evening practising over and over again.

He was working on a particularly difficult pattern that looked like bubbles rising from a cauldron when the man from the market sat down opposite him.

'You are wasting your time. You will never be a scholar; you have a different destiny.'

Jamal looked up and shivered a little. He still didn't trust the man from the market. Then he realised that he didn't even know his name. Jamal only ever thought of him as 'the man from the market'. He would need to ask Ahmed what it was. Ahmed was definitely not a scholar, but he was great for knowing names and dates and gossip.

'Thank you for your advice, but it's everyone's duty to study and learn as much about the world as he can.' Jamal hoped that would make the man from the market leave him alone. His answer hadn't actually been rude, but it very nearly was.

'Some destinies are more glorious than scholarship. Wouldn't you like to have a glorious destiny?'

What was this man talking about? Jamal wondered if it would be OK to say he had an important appointment somewhere else.

'If you don't want a glorious destiny, maybe I can persuade you.'

Jamal thought that the man from the market was really creepy. He talked in a scary way even when he wasn't saying anything that was actually scary.

'Do you remember when you first came here? Do you remember that you brought a cylinder with you?'

Jamal did remember.

'Did you ever wonder why it was so important?'

Jamal was suddenly interested. He had learnt that the ghosts and the spirits weren't real but he still didn't know what was in the canisters that he had seen before he came to the city.

'It was a poison gas canister. An illegal weapon. An illegal weapon that the police would be very interested in.'

'Do you still have it?' asked Jamal. 'If you do, shouldn't we take it to the police?'

'Oh, I've still got it,' said the man. 'And it's got your fingerprints all over it. I bet the police would be very interested in that. Don't you think so?'

If what the man from the market said was true, then the police would be interested. Jamal couldn't understand why the man from the market sounded as if he was threatening him.

'So, are you going to accept your destiny? Or shall I tell the police where you have hidden the poison gas?'

Now Jamal understood why the man sounded as if he was threatening him. It was because he was.

'Come, I'll show you something.'

He walked out of the room and Jamal followed him. They went to a hidden part of the compound, well away from the school and the dormitories.

'Come in here,' the man from the market said. 'I have made a coat that will fit you perfectly.'

Suddenly Jamal thought he knew what the man was talking about. But he wished he didn't.

'I told you once before that the army is our enemy, and your destiny could be to destroy that enemy.'

Jamal was very frightened. More frightened than when he first heard the silence. More frightened than when he met his grandfather. More frightened even than when the people had called him a witch. This man was mad.

'I need to think about what's right,' said Jamal.

'You can think. But you must think here. You have a choice: accept your destiny or go to jail.'

That wasn't a choice, Jamal thought. That wasn't a choice at all. This madman wanted him to die and Jamal didn't want that at all.

He tried to think what else he could do. Jamal knew that he could move faster than this madman. He could run away from him. He could run back to the dump where he'd be safe. Mham would hide him and Jamal knew that once you were hidden on the dump no one could find you.

That wouldn't work. He would be OK, but he remembered that Ahmed had touched the cylinder as well. He couldn't run away and leave Ahmed.

What else? What else? Jamal needed another idea.

He wondered if he could go along with the plan and then run to the police.

No, that wouldn't work. This man would have thought of that.

What else?

'Well, boy, have you thought?'

'Yes, sir. I know just what to do.'

Jamal picked up the canister and flung it at the man from the market. Then he ran as fast as he could, dodging under the man's arm while he was looking at the canister. Almost at once, Jamal was out of the room, skidding right and left and heading for the main compound.

'It's a bomb!' shouted Jamal. 'There's a bomb. We've got to get out. *There's a bomb!*'

The End

Acknowledgements

I'd like to thank all the people who have helped me in the making of this book. The people who've checked my facts and checked my spelling and who have let me ignore them while I've been writing. You have been wonderful and I couldn't have done it without you.